Foun

and

Other Misfits

Poems and Tales

Estelle Gilson

GARDEN OAK PRESS
Rainbow, California

Garden Oak Press
1953 Huffstatler St., Suite A
Rainbow, CA 92028
760 728-2088
gardenoakpress.com
gardenoakpress@gmail.com

First published by Garden Oak Press on May 15, 2020.

ISBN-13: 978-1-7323753-7-6

Library of Congress Control Number: 2020935618

Printed in the United States of America

The views expressed in this collection of poems and tales are solely those of the writer and do not necessarily reflect the views of the Publisher, and the Publisher hereby disclaims any responsibility for them.

Nel mezzo del cammin di nostra vita
mi ritrovai per una selva oscura,
ché la diritta via era smarrita.

—DANTE ALIGHIERI

Out of the woods – not yet in Paradise.

— ESTELLE GILSON

CONTENTS

Foundlings

I Dream of Foundlings	5
The Doll	6
You, Anger	7
The Pear	8
Wet at the Gate	9
Electra	10
Ode to WFAN	11
The Swim	12
A Daughter is a Stone in the Heart	13
Toll Roads	14
Here	15
Glass of Water at 3 a.m.	16
Visit on My Mother's Birthday	17
Please, Mamma	18
Buzzing Universe	19
It's Not How I Love You	20
For Saul	21
The Height of the Delicious	22
Silver Rose	23
Haunted	24
Little Sister	25
My mother admonished me not to cry	26
My Name is Mimi	27
My Wild Thing	28
Onion	29
Recorded	30
Shopping List	31
Divine Comedy	32
To a Photophobic Poet	33
Sometimes I Think	34
To Certain Esteemed Poets	35
Spring	36
Mushrooms Are Better Than Poetry	37
Flame	38
Sorry, Jenny	38
Layle	39
Vesuvius	40
My Parents Took Me to the Yiddish Theater	42
My Own Moon	43
Geminis	44
Psychotherapy	46

Other Misfits

The Baby's Room	49
Making My Own Movie	51
Why I Became a Writer So Late in Life	53
The Moment	54
Handsome Dog	55
The Juggler	58
How the First Family Spent Mother's Day	60
Tests	64
Hotel	66
Cold Supper	68
Without Love	79
The Man Who Sold His Mother	87
Black and White	93
How to Lay a Flagstone Terrace	112
Piazza's Back in the Lineup	121
ABOUT THE WRITER	131
ACKNOWLEDGMENTS	132
CREDITS	133

Foundlings
and
Other Misfits

Poems and Tales

Estelle Gilson

GARDEN OAK PRESS

Foundlings

I Dream of Foundlings

I dream of foundlings
silent babes
in darkened rooms
breathing their innocence.

I dream my infant son
compact, talc scented
warm in my arms
sucking my poisoned breast.

I dream the stripling child I lost
mutely watching copulation on a screen.
Neither of us knows how old he is.

I dream the infant girl waking to hunger's rage
whose mother climbs Escher steps and never reaches her.
She will dream of foundlings.

The Doll

She was born in June
Dolls have birthdays too
Festive days
when the Gods little girls barely dream of
bend low
to make them smile

and was immediately unloved
Perhaps a boy was wanted
Perhaps she came too early
or was imperfect
It's true, her sawdust leaked a little
and her cheeks were setting suns
but she cried mamma
The Gods make bitter mistakes

So she was lifted from her box
and it seemed like love
Even the Gods were fooled
to see her pressed so fiercely
against those tiny breasts

Now, of course, it's too late
Crushed for the other's loneliness
torn for her wounds
there is no sawdust left
Still, dangling from the sleeper's hand
she cries mamma

You, Anger

You, anger, burn
tear at rusting bars
that don't give
chew on the leather heart
that lives
in there with you.

Prisoner and guard, we
never loved and never may
Concealment was the game
the pretense of our decades.

The child pinned beneath your yellow eyes
was too afraid to scream.

The girl sang coloratura in the sunshine
you stilled her voice with shame.

The matron fed her hungry first,
fattened you, then choked.

Too well you sowed the poison tree
still keepers could not answer to your end.

Anger.
Unmerciful anger.
The tired old woman would call you friend.

The Pear

The pear,
bright green buttocks in the air
is stuck in the toilet

The mother
salivating, would salvage the pear
but is ashamed.

The father would flush the pear
but is afraid it will lodge in a pipe
and render his tenancy unpleasant.

As if it is a stranger's fruit
neither touches it.

Wet at the Gate

Wet at the ghetto gate
without clothes, speech or food
I am taken in, taught never to be naked, speechless
or wet again.

I think it love 'til the cashier asks a price
 — teaching learning never ends —
then swallow understanding.
Hold it in.

The street is paved with glittering chips that blacken
beneath my feet.

Deep in the ladies room the sick and maimed plead
 — sweet splash of women—
curtained stalls are taken
I hold it in.

Atop broad marble steps lit with flame
red velvet footmen scan extended cards —
admit only ticket holders.

I stumble toward the gate
and let the learning out.

Electra

My father is a white bone
fixed beneath my feet
Earth and gore
stop his mouth.

I am the white stone
fixed on his grave
feeding on the sun's blood
learning to kill.

Ode to WFAN

Sleepless
I reach for the earpiece.

It's not quiet I seek
not syncopation
or information.

Money riding on Giants and Jets
spit on the Yankees, shit on the Mets
smash-mouth players, sticks and pucks
GMs, owners, coaches that suck

efflux of wakefulness — voices hell-bent
two-centsing ways sports millions are spent.

Anger is my lullaby.

The Swim

No laps for myself
no "personal best"
"because it's there"
or every stroke an Olympian
for them dry at the sides
with their notebooks and their noddings
their clocks and their clickings.

Water stiffens against my arms.
Soon I drift
pretending innocence.

A Daughter is a Stone in the Heart

Hard to be a stone.
Harder only
to be a stone
in her heart.

What can sing in a stone
spit by raging Lyssa
abandoned to anneal,
choke the way of seedlings?

Can a stone shout its faith?
Cry its afflictions?

Yet a stone
struck against its grain
fractures
as does a heart.

Toll Roads

My mother said, "I'm sorry it's so late
and you have to go to work tomorrow."

She said, "It was lovely.
I don't deserve it."

"And you have to pay a toll
 I don't even have a car."

"I should ask you in for coffee
but its too late, isn't it?"

Next to you I worry that it's late
and you have to work tomorrow.
I can't think why you love me.
When you pay for dinner I'm a beggar.
Should I ask you in for a drink?

I thought I had strangled her.

Here

There is nothing between me and there
yet I am always here
now
cross-legged on the bed, playing the flute
is never now.

Nothing around me but there
yet I linger here
the regurgitation
of an unrelenting tide
foundering in its fury.

I reach for there
yet I'm fixed here
shrieking
and bloodstained
in an ancient Eden
a murderer tethered to then.

Glass of Water at 3 a.m.

I too am circumscribed by a body
endless and tense
that shapes me
lifts me toward death.

I would transcend my body,
spill and sparkle,
reflect the cool moon
slide new slopes
explore lowest places
and be lost.

I would escape the gaping mouth.

Visit on My Mother's Birthday

No need to remind you
Do not go gently.
You did nothing gentle in my life.
Not one caress
but carapaced in blinding need
I thought love.

Honor, you insisted
and despised my gifts.
Sympathy, you cried,
spit curses,
speared my fleeing back
then wept to be alone.

Each of us at the threshold
awaits an open door.
We will embrace
and pass in rage.

Please, Mamma

Don't die yet, mamma.
Please.
I'm just learning to hate.
Don't cheat me again.

Tell me everyone else has husbands, sons, brothers,
but you have only me.
Tell me what you need and what I bring are not the same.
Make me Mary's shopper,
Sarah's chauffeur.
I'm only 60.
Spit when I refuse.

Then go back with me, mamma.
I need to go back and scream.
I need to bite your breast,
cling to your ankles,
I need to hit you and call you names.
I need to hate you, mamma.

Don't die yet, please.
I'm empty, mamma.
Hold me.

Buzzing Universe

I remember fly paper
at every table
how it hung
mustard
yellow
from
uncertain
fans
how it
dangled
crusted
coruscated
beady
black
ugly
with
strugglers
and
dead

There are no flies where I live now
in sealed and sheltered grace.

Whatever made me remember fly paper?

It's Not How I Love You

It's not how I love you
it's how you love me
that counts

Moon loves tide
to govern its flow

Moth seeks flame
to die in its glow

Beauty holds mirror
which never lying, lies

Saint needs sinner
to rise

It's not how I love you that counts
I know only one way

For Saul

I have found you everywhere,
on my left every morning in bed,
in this kitchen you've never seen,
helping me search spice shelves for cumin.

In an auto, never yours,
on palm-lined streets you never knew,
you find me parking spaces
when I call on you.

Where we loved
the house is empty.
Willows mourn yellow,
beeches grieve in brown
beyond the cedar you planted
at the muddy curve in the stream.
The gravel we chose,
just the right size for walking barefoot,
has vanished beneath green sprouts
that refuse to relinquish living.

I doubt you went gentle that night.
Quickly, silently, yes,
but rage was more your style,
so I thought you'd like to know about the sprouts.

The Height of the Delicious

with a nod to Oliver Wendell Holmes

I cooked some dishes once on a time
        in a wondrous hungry mood
and thought as usual, guests would say,
        My dear, these are so good.

Courses rich and courses smooth
        I nibbled as I stirred all
albeit I'm a slender gal
        and never wear a girdle.

I called my husband and he came;
        how kind of him to do so.
Our contract doesn't specify
        he's Friday to my Crusoe.

"These to the freezer," I called out
        and in my humorous way
I added (he just loves my puns)
        "There'll be Jack Frost to pay."

He took the tray and I watched.
        Oh, this is far too riche!
Pushing aside the wrap, he sneaked
        a fingerful of quiche.

He smiled, then finished: on to ragout,
        herbs and wines and meats.
That downed, he loosed his belt again
        and attacked the next of treats.

With baked Alaska gone, then mousse,
        I heard a sudden split,
"Is it waistband or arteries, darling," I cried
        as he tumbled in a fit.

Ten days and nights, with sleepless eye
        I nursed that dyspeptic man
and since, I've never dared to cook
        as delicious as I can.

Silver Rose

Heut haben Sie ein altes Weib aus mir gemacht!
I'm not talking to my hairdresser
complaining that my teenage lover
won't want to sleep with me anymore.
I'm talking to my mirror, telling it
it's scrolled my years
sucked the marrow from my bones
corrugated my face
seized my shoulders
stiffened my neck
and
withered,
set me adrift
to make much of time.

Haunted

Rome. How old were you –
11, 12 when we shlepped you
from church to church ?
Daddy had arrived with a list.
Once you and I skipped out for gelato.

How many pilasters and pillars
braces and buttresses
how many cupolas, arches
vaults and domes did we see?
How many martyrs and saints
Christs and Marys?

The *Pietà*.

Too weak to shave,
too distant on your white sheets
for me to do other than kiss your bearded face,
you smiled when you said, "enough already,"
and I smiled back.

Little Sister

I am in a hotel room in a strange city
on the eve of your granddaughter's wedding.

We didn't meet at the airport this time,
dragging suitcases behind and waving at each other,
giddy with release from mundane chores.

We would be whispering now
bed to bed in this gaudy room
recalling early loves
gathering fragments of loss
doing "remember?"
giggling over our little girl years
when we kicked and quarreled on the iron-legged couch
that yawned for us every night.

Little sister, deepest vessel of memory,
once again the smiling child in a high chair
offering bread but unable to say my name.

I am without you in a hotel room in a strange city
on the eve of your granddaughter's wedding.

My mother admonished me not to cry

My mother admonished me not to cry.
I had a good life, she said,
though we both knew she hadn't.
I cried.

My father had no time to prepare anyone
or dole out instructions, though I doubt
he would have wanted to.
I cried.

One by one those I journeyed with passed
each into their own silence.
One by one I cried,

then learned to live
my own silence,
retravel journeys
alone.

I'll tell my son not to cry.
I've had a good life, I'll say,
He'll probably cry anyway.
Then, perhaps –
it takes time –
he'll come across one of the dreadful puns
                    we've foisted on each other,
and grudgingly groan again.

My Name is Mimi

with apologies to Puccini

When I email you I'm Lu
– because I don't know you
and I don't want you to know me.

I don't want you to know me
because I want to be free
and have the upper hand.

I want to have the upper hand
because I need to know where I stand
in every transaction,

because every transaction
evokes a reaction
and sometimes I lose control,

and if I lose control
and write something too blue,
I'd rather you were mad at Lu
than at me.

My Wild Thing

They say if a poet you want to be
invite your fiercest fear to tea.

All the lions and tigers were out of town.
I got a hairy beast with a wicked frown.

"Boo," she yelled through saber-sharp teeth.
I fell to floor— could hardly breathe.

We had egg salad, pickles and good white wine.
I spoke when I thought she looked more benign.

"Are you nasty and mean, all my worst fears?"
I boldly asked, on the verge of tears.

"I am," she roared, all smirky with bile,
then shockingly added, "Now honey, smile."

"But you're hairy and scary and dangerous too."
"Still, now we've met, I can never hurt you."

Then up she leaps and dances me 'round
and we whirl and we laugh and fall to the ground.

Then we talk and we talk 'til she has to go home,
and look, everyone, I wrote a poem.

Onion

How like an onion am I now,
who once was warm and tender.
Papery scales my pulp surround,
gone my peach hued splendor.

Juicy substance no longer flows
through giving fleshy texture.
Sodden eyes sans fiery glow
mock the siren gesture.

Gone the psyche's curvy bulb,
thick layered with acrid stress,
once crisp and nervy, now scant and dull
stripped of sting and zest.

Exiguous in core and coat,
roots and end so near,
old *Allium cepas,* this poet notes,
bring only themselves to tears.

Recorded

in memory of Gabriel Preil

What is Shostakovitch doing here in San Diego
as the largest moon of the year
pauses above the patient Pacific?
His spiky clarinets jabber in Yiddish,
clowns quickstep atop fierce plumes
belched by a murderous furnace.
Somehow I wanted to believe he could find peace
in this agreeable climate
but his cellos drum relentlessly
and bitter laughter is eternal.
He is recorded.

Let's take a minute to think about Preil's music.
How it asks to be free.
The Grand Duke of New York saunters through town,
observes, assesses, writes, "it's raining,"
notes where sparrows live.
In Jerusalem and the Bronx
he shakes loose smiles at his own desires,
celebrates now
and masters the praise of apples.
He is recorded.

They tell me I too am recorded
and won't be heard in elevators.

Shopping List

Sipping Fernet Branca
tempered with sweet vermouth as I write,
and ice, of course.
Usually Scotch
but this evening — I don't know why
a bittersweet concoction.

What do I need?

I went to Brooklyn College — free
Ate at the Automat.
Three vegetables — five cents each.
Always baked beans — two whatevers.
Also Nedick's nickel orange "drink,"
their hotdogs.
Once on a hot summer sidewalk in 1949
I drove people at Nedicks on Broadway crazy
in my 20-year-old blondness with my black boyfriend.
Drove my parents crazy.
Then I drove the boyfriend crazy.
Turns out he was married.

I live in a classy senior residence now,
shop around the corner at Bristol Farms,
"an upscale grocery chain in California,"
according to Wikipedia.
So many imported
exotic
organic
free range
fair trade
foods.

What do I need?

Divine Comedy

I never envied her until I past 90
and began thinking about heaven.

It's spring.
I'm twelve, a violinist,
he's fourteen, blows the mournful oboe
Jesu, Joy of Man's Desiring
and doesn't know I exist.
Through the rehearsal room's tall windows
I can see the sky
deep blue, cloud blown, radiant,
a sky of miracles and promises
in which haloed Saints, holy prophets
are borne aloft.
When a breeze light as breath brushes my arm
I want something I'm not sure exists.

The story goes that she was eight
when he fell in love with her
and he was nine.
He turned it into a very long story
of unconsummated love
plus some other things.
Did she even know about him?
She married someone else.
Nevertheless he awarded her purity, intellect, eternal glory
and a seat next to Rachel
on a petal of the white rose
in the highest heaven.

Ribono shel olam!!!
That's the only heaven I know.

To a Photophobic Poet

Let the jingly delicious Emperor
the invisible
silent
headliner
set you straight
on the whattage of your words

Sometimes I Think

Sometimes I think and think
and don't know what to think.

Sometimes I dream and dream
and don't know when I dreamed.

Sometimes I love and love
and don't know who I love.

Sometimes I weep and rage.
For that I have a name.

To Certain Esteemed Poets

I feel ashamed
not to understand you.

That's not exactly what I mean.
I'm ashamed to make it known
that I don't understand you.

Not the precise truth either,
because here I am confessing to you
that I don't understand.

I guess what I mean is that I trust
you would understand
not understanding.

Or is it, esteemed poets,
that I cannot understand
because I cannot command?

Spring

There is a quivering in spring
that joys the heart
with the certainty of miracles:

crocuses rise
through crusty ice

phoebes alight
on remembered nests

peepers sing
love's lullabies

dry sticks redeem
the colorless world.

Fail when life is greening
the sun climbing?
Life presumes tomorrow

yet when sap and humors rise
where's gravity?

Beginnings are not promises
innocence no protection
tenderness perilous.

Last night a squirrel found the phoebe nest.

Mushrooms Are Better Than Poetry

for chia hui

Mushrooms can be eaten raw,
poetry not.
Mushrooms can be eaten cooked,
poetry not.
Mushrooms can be made into soup,
poetry not.
Soup never fails body or soul.
Poetry maybe.

Flame

He came on a wind
stretched thin and golden as a blown flame
igniting embers of lust.

My ancient limbs remember
unfurl their willingness
pulse, arc, rise,
I will my breath to reach his mouth,
inhale the salt of love.

My eyes see nothing.
My tongue seeks in vain.
My body sinks unweighted.
I bury my flaming face.

Sorry, Jenny

I'll never wear a red dress with a purple hat,
eat pickles, hoard beer mats, or spit just for yuks.
The middle-age and weary dream of that,
I'm 80, I tried it, it sucks.

Layle

for our Wednesday Poetry Class on the eve of spring

I didn't walk well
speak well
see or hear well.
My husband was ill.
Winter was hell
not flaming
numbing.
I'd lost a friend
without a word
without a tear.

Where to seek her?
Hear her voice?

Not aloft
lauding immortality
to denizens
of generic heaven.

Not in fields
or spring gardens
singing lilacs
into her arms.

In water
cool waters unstirred by currents
I strike keen shards
and answers flow.

Vesuvius

"Why do people live on active volcanoes?
For food.
Volcanic soil grows
tomatoes, pistachios, figs, grapes.
People take high-risk gambles
for the basic things of life."

Even for love.
We sail
the level sea
ascend Napoli's
terraced slopes
awash
in Christ's tears
to reach the jagged rim.

"The trail circles the crater.
Refreshments are found at the summit.
At the summit, you can buy ornaments made of lava,
buy a guidebook, or just peek into the crater."

Vulcan lies
below
peaceful

pieceful
as in appearing
a quiet whole
yet wholey lying
seething
and lying
in wait.

I quiver
alongside you
in the queue
atop Vesuvius
wondering
am I the only one
who feels
trembling
beneath
her feet?

My Parents Took Me
to the Yiddish Theater

I didn't understand a word
but this is what happened:
the curtain went up.
There was a girl.
There was a boy.
Right away I figured out what was supposed to happen.
Otherwise, why write a show?
Love!
I could hardly wait.
But there was a problem.
She wanted him,
but he didn't want her.
She yelled at him.
He yelled at her.
The relatives yelled at each other.
Someone fired a gun.
How this worked, don't ask me
but now he wanted her
only she didn't want him anymore.
He yelled at her.
She yelled at him.
The relatives yelled at each other.
Someone else fired a gun.
So many Jews have guns?
But now thank God
another miracle:
they want each other.
I sigh, lean forward.
The curtain comes down.

My Own Moon

In feathered hope and warmth
in stillness of wordless breath

locked
ankle to ankle
knee to knee
wrists to chest

I wake womb wound.

Geminis

1

Actualized personalities
perfect dualities

talents
balanced

yin and yang lie
belly over eye

twinned bliss crowned
backs circled round

single soul
perfect whole

Eternally a ring
Their peace I sing

2

Juney
is a Gemini

her own twin
but not yang and yin

selves don't match
can't latch

into each other
sister or brother

black and white
dark and light

Ys issued breach
wrong ends of each

now bulge and cram
swell and slam

howl and roll
misshape her soul

two tortured bags
here she bulges, there she sags

give, take, yes, no
love, hate, stop, go

Peace forever denied
Wretched Juney, for thee I cry

Psychotherapy

I spent
you don't want to know how many
years
and
dollars
on psychotherapy
and discovered
that all you bastards are innocent.
I'm the one ruining my life.
Now what?
Hemlock?
Screw you, Socrates!

Other Misfits

The Baby's Room

The baby's room was dark. There was no sound in it except his breathing. She tiptoed in, found the table next to the baby's bed and started the phonograph playing softly. It would be the last time she would come to him at night. The family had decided that weeks ago. Now that the last night had come they wanted it over with quickly. They had sent her in early. It was nearly dinner time. Outside the baby's room they waited restlessly.

The baby was nearly two—still soft and compact and plump with a round face, very dark round eyes, and a sad and serious way. He smelled of warm powder and diapers and sleep. And the smell was sweet.

In the dark room the baby whimpered. The sound startled her. She realized the record had finished playing and began it again. The baby whimpered once more and then was still.

For the past several months, they had been getting him ready for tonight. The drops were bitter-tasting but he had learned to take them one at a time because they hugged him and kissed him and told him what a wonderful baby, what a good little boy, he was when he swallowed one. And in his large sad eyes they could see he loved to hear them say it. He always fell asleep immediately after taking the drops.

The baby's room opened off the dining room. Its closed door was framed in a rectangle of light that spread thinly against the adjacent surfaces. The sounds of footsteps, voices, silver, and dishes rode into the room on the light. But the sounds of hunger penetrated even further into the room.

They weren't being in the least subdued. "C'mon," Karen called. "What's taking you so long?" The rest of them merely murmured. But in the darkened room she felt their derision.

It wasn't her baby. Why did she have to do it? Why did she have to give him the six drops instead of the usual two tonight? That's not really doing anything. And it had to be done. They had all decided that. Decided together.

Outside the baby's room where there was light and food and wine and human voices it seemed easy. "Hurry up, will you? I'm hungry." Karen again. She opened the door. She stood in the light with one hand on the oaken buffet, her dirty blonde hair hanging along her face and thin neck. Her legs were bare. Her feet flat against the floor in leather sandals looked large and dark and resolute. She stared into the baby's room. The baby whimpered again and Karen shut the door.

It had to be done. There was no sense letting him go on. He would always be a problem to them and to himself.

The phonograph stopped again. She tried to restart the record but couldn't find the tone arm in the dark. The baby's sobs became more frequent. Her hands groped along the table top. Nothing beneath her fingers felt familiar. When she touched the phonograph, it seemed to lose substance as if slipping off into a void. The baby's cries grew louder.

Someone knocked on the door. "Get it over with. We want to eat." The voice struck at her chest. The baby was crying constantly now. She leaned over the crib rails and picked him up. He was wearing fuzzy yellow pajamas that covered even his feet. She held him in her right hand. His weight rested on her forearm. Instinctively, he leaned forward so that his head was on her shoulder and his body pressed against her chest. His breath blew lightly against her neck. His warmth flooded her breasts. His smells burned high in her nostrils. "What's the matter?" she whispered.

He lifted his head and looked at her. "What's the matter?" she repeated.

"Fatht, fatht," he said and leaned against her again. What did he mean? His heart was beating rapidly against hers.

"You scared?" she asked.

The baby sighed.

"Would you like to take your medicine now?"

"Yeth," he said in his serious way.

Suddenly she sobbed, put him back into the crib and turned to stare at the door.

Outside in the light, she could hear them moving. They were restless and hungry.

Making My Own Movie
for JF

Yesterday, I became the heroine of my own movie. Not that I was ever in a movie except for the picture show that's been my life — the one in which I accelerate from zero to 60 in nothing flat — boxed in with my dear old ma who never lets me forget the years she spent diapering me. Really, me 60 and her 90 and she still reminds me so I'm sure you can figure out the plot, this story of my life that I never wrote, not even the dialogue — that is until yesterday — because I was so busy following her script and doing for her what she needed done — my mother never wanted anything from me — wanting is mean, inconsiderate and selfish and my mother was always too good and kind and totally noble to want. That's what I learned from her — Don't want — Even before I got pinned into that first diaper — Because you won't get. Her milk made me sick. I should have known right then and there she'd hold it against me the rest of my life, which is the same as forever, lousy allergic kid. My mother's the one they named the insurance after — Ms No-Fault of 1900 — but I wasn't smart enough at zero and I didn't get smart enough or maybe mad enough 'til I hit 60, when I finally noticed all those cities and towns, streams and mountains rushing by. And me strapped into the back seat of the car under a pile of shoulds and oughts. Look ma, no temptations! Boy, was I good! And kind, the way a lousy allergic daughter whose mother had worked so hard diapering her should be. So there we were, two totally noble women, neither wanting a thing. But one needed. Vacations and trips and phone calls and letters and cocktails and lunches and hats and coats and pocketbooks and consolation and pity and apologies and coals in Newcastle, meaning aspirin in a nursing home. And only from me. So you can see how I never got to be a heroine, that is until yesterday.

Is that you? My eyes are terrible I can't see. Where were you Tuesday? Did you bring the aspirin?

I was sick.

51

You look all right now. They don't tell you anything here. They are the masters, we are the slaves. Here comes my aide.

I thought you can't see.

A bitch. Smile. What is your name dear? Josephine, this is my daughter. Isn't she lovely. She took such good care of me 'til I got here. Yes, see you later. Give me the aspirin.

I don't have it.

You can't bring me a bottle of aspirin?

They give you aspirin here.

They hate you if you ask for anything.

I spoke to the nurse.

A daughter is a stone in the heart.

I wheel her chair around and push it it forward, when suddenly the tires are clinging to the floor. My mother has put the brakes on. The chair, not herself. She is screaming.

And eight cylinders of gas explode. The soundtrack of my movie. A motor whines into gear. The picture starts. 60. A needle twitches, inches up to 70, 80 and 90 are possible. Wheels scream over iron bridges. Cities and towns, streams and mountains flash by. I want to grab the wheel, feel the brake under my foot. I want to stop, get out, know where I am. I want to feel wet and cold, hot and parched. I want to climb and fall and get up again. I want to take and be taken, give and be given. I want vacations and trips and cocktails and lunches and coats and pocketbooks and consolation and apologies and coals in Newcastle.

So I bend over and kiss my mother goodby. Then I turn and walk away. Towards the camera. Towards you. I can't see you or hear you. But I know you're watching, cheering, applauding my victory. So I smile and wave. And get larger and larger as I move closer to you.

Why I Became a Writer So Late in Life

Oh yes, writing is good. Grandpa was a writer. Tolstoy was a writer. So was Shakespeare. So was Hilda somebody or other. See? Only 10 years old and she has a book of poems published.

I am young, but old enough to read and write. I am on a bench on the boardwalk sitting next to someone, probably Uncle. My back is against the back of the bench, which is on the street side of the boardwalk and my legs, my humiliating little girls' legs, stick straight out in front of me.

What kind of day is it? The sun is warm. Though I can no longer see it on my skin, I can still see it — in broad horizontals below me through brown, splintery slats — on the pale pitted grittiness of sand lying between iron rails. And the rest is blue. Sea and sky. With the wind made visible by whiteness. By spume and tilted sails.

I guess I had a pad and pencil with me. Or someone did. And I felt like writing a poem. Why? Do poets ever know? Even real poets? Maybe it was a counterpoint — the frivolousness of the sunbeams against the persistence of the waves? Maybe the grace of the distant boats. I had never seen a sailboat close up. Maybe just the pastel danciness of what lay before my eager eyes.

Whatever! I did it, I wrote a poem

"Very nice."

"What a clever child to write a poem. Only you used 'blue' before. See? On the second line. So use something else here. And 'ship' - that's wrong. It should be 'boat'. And the last two lines don't rhyme. See? Let Uncle fix it up for you."

And make it perfect.

And have it typed.

And show it off.

Over your name, of course.

After all, writing is good. Grandpa was a writer. Tolstoy was a writer. So was Shakespeare.

And so was God.

Though they spared me that.

The Moment

She has kissed him goodnight in the dark and they have turnedfrom each other.

On her right, the whirring clock, infinite as the universe, casts up numerals cold and white as the small moon high in a winter sky.

Her toes are icy.

How long ago?

Now she is sweating, hunched and in pain, deep in the trough of the double bed and the woman, large, thick, still, carved from some sarcophagus, head pressed against the headboard is on her right.

On the left, the man's blue smooth-clothed back still curves away. The trough is narrow. She must lie tightly on her side.

Then a pain sears her right thigh, she turns to the left, rising high and moaning. She is afraid to touch the other bodies. The woman's — colorless, rigid, mountainous, a monolith, a caryatid, an omen, unyielding. A woman by the brown hair spreading over the pillow. The hair of Medusa, a harpy, a fury.

The man — younger, warm, breathing, unknowing, uncaring.

In the trough she is curled at the level of their backs. Knees drawn up, ankles twisted, her hands taut against her wrists, wrists against her chest, head bent — her bones walling her heart.

Why is the woman there? Which of them is the intruder? She cannot remember whose bed it is.

The woman is waiting. The woman is watching. The woman's eyes are white stones.

The man moves and his warmth pours into the trough. For a moment, a mere moment, ancient longings transform him and she recognizes the woman and knows why she is there. Then the moment is gone.

Still the woman lies flat and heavy, unmoving and unmoved, silent with that furious hair and eyes that are stones but can see.

The man must remain who he is.

54

Handsome Dog

It was late afternoon when she got home. The top lock wasn't secured. She felt a flick of annoyance. He never remembered, not even since the burglary. Then turning the key she forgave him. Maybe he was inside waiting for her. She slid her suitcase through the door, and heard the phone ringing. She took a step towards it, then retreated and pressed silently against the wall. Two, three rings, four. He didn't pick up. She answered in the study.

"Mrs. Marek?" It was Lionel Arles. "Is Bruce home?"

"I'm just back from out of town, Mr. Arles. Isn't he at the office?"

"Haven't seen him all day. Well, that's not important, just tell him when he gets back that the old lady signed on. He'll know. He's a charmer, that husband of yours, Mrs. Marek," Arles laughed.

"Thank you," she said.

When she hung up, she was afraid to open the bedroom door. No one was in the room. For a change, his underwear on the floor, the pin stripe suit crumpled on the bed, were a relief. It didn't last long. She knew the problem was in her mind. He hadn't said he'd be home. It was the lock. But now she felt betrayed. Found herself wondering how old that lady was.

In the kitchen, the familiar anger flared. Crumbs and puddles. Seven days of cigarettes bloated brown in coffee. The dog chained to the table pawing and whining. "C'mon Antony, I'll take you out." She secured the muzzle around the Dalmatian's head, chose the long, leather training lead and attached it to the choke.

The sun hadn't set It was still warm. There were people on the street. It occurred to her she might meet him if he were coming home now. "Heel, Antony," she snapped the lead, keeping the dog's head at her left flank. She passed teenagers in long patches of light, lovers against lampposts, workers sauntering in the promise of the new season. They irritated her. "Heel." Beyond the rounded

55

greenery of the park, a sharp edged storm darkened the horizon.

"Does he bite, lady?"

She was tired of the question. "He nibbles," she answered flatly, remembering when the answer was new and she used to smile to say it. Why did they think he wore a muzzle?.

When had the dog begun to snap? She tried to remember, but her mind kept coming back to him. She'd left a message on the machine last night. He could at least have cleaned up his mess. "Can I pet him? He's wagging his tail. That means he likes me."

"It doesn't mean anything. C'mon Antony," the lead snapped sharply.

He'd promised. He was always promising. A block from the park, she spotted Ted Reiser coming toward her with that yappy schnauzer. She held the dog close and kept her eyes down, hoping the old man would pass her. He could babble for an hour while the lousy hound twisted herself around everything in sight. "Hi," Reiser smiled. "Heard you were away."

"Sit, Antony." The dog, watching the schnauzer, didn't move. "Sit, I said. Yes."

"Your husband said your mother was sick. I hope she's better. He looked so worried. Such a nice man. Helped my wife take out the garbage yesterday."

"The garbage," she said, yanking the dog to his feet. "My mother died. We've got to get to the park."

"Sorry to hear it." Reiser looked down at the dog. "Still muzzled, eh? It always upsets me to see it. I can remember when he was so quiet. He's such a beautiful animal."

"Handsome is as handsome does." Another of the things she used to smile to say. In the days when she smiled. The schnauzer was sniffing at her shoes.

He hadn't even come out for the funeral. "We've got this big deal going down. There's no way I can leave town."

"He's wagging his tail. I bet he's basically friendly."

"I know. Everyone thinks I'm mean and he's friendly. Excuse me," she tried to pass him. "It looks like rain."

Reiser held his ground. "I can't believe he'd hurt me. He has such soft, brown eyes. Besides, he knows I like him. Dogs and children can sense things like that." He stepped closer to the dog. Antony growled softly, then turned his head away.

"Here, Antony. Nice Antony," the old man extended the back of his hand cautiously.

The dog's ears were low against his head, his neck stretched forward. Then, suddenly, Antony roared, lunged and snapped. Ted Reiser leaped back. She pulled the dog tightly to her side.

"Omigod." Reiser was pale, breathless. "I don't believe it."

"I tried to tell you." Her voice was sharp. "Do you think I like to keep him muzzled?"

"No, sorry, OK." He had trouble getting his breath. "Well, I've got to get going. My condolences about your mother and I hope your sister's better. I'll see you around."

"My sister?"

"She passed out or something, last night. Maybe because of your mother. Met them in the elevator. Said he was taking her home. Come along, Bananas, I feel a drop of rain." Reiser untangled the schnauzer from a parking meter.

A clap of thunder broke overhead. For a moment she felt the sound was inside her.

He hadn't changed. He'd never change.

Reiser looked back at her and hesitated.

"I don't have a sister," she said at last, but by then, he was gone.

It took only a minute to reach the park. The grass and trees were no longer green, but stony as the sky.

"OK, Antony," she whispered, pulling the long lead through her closed left hand. The end dangled from it like a whip. Lightning streaked.

"Down," she called. The dog stood rigidly.

"Down." The loop hung from her right hand now. She swung it against the dog's back. Again and again. "Down, you bastard."

The Juggler

She is wearing the mask when from a passing bus she thinks she sees her son juggling knives in front of the museum. She removes the mask to press her face against the window.

It can't be her son. Her son lives in a distant place. Too distant to visit, he says. And he is there now. She is certain because it is Sunday and they will phone him that night at nine. They phone him every Sunday at nine. They take turns, she and her husband. Tonight it is her husband's turn. The conversation will be brief. Their son is a busy man in that distant place.

The window fogs with her breath. She cannot see clearly. When she tries to replace the mask, it no longer fits.

All day her face is hot.

"It's funny," she begins, "I thought I saw our son juggling knives in front of the museum this afternoon."

"Funny?" her husband says.

"It couldn't have been him." She twitches slightly to ease the pressure of the mask against her temple. "He's up there waiting for you to call. If he were in the city. he would have let us know."

"Who cares where he is?" her husband says.

"It's nice to stay in touch. And to hear his voice," she says. The mask fits comfortably now. It is even possible to improvise. "I was thinking I would ask him down for the holidays."

"He won't come. He never does."

"No harm in asking. In fact we have to. How will he know we want to see him, unless we say so?" Her voice is almost gay.

"He doesn't want to see us. It's more than a year now. And he never phones."

She knows her husband is remembering his eye surgery; one eye behind a metal shield, both eyes moist. But her smile is steady. "He doesn't have to phone us. He knows we call every week."

The man glares at her. "If we miss a week, does he call to see if we're alive?"

"He's busy."

"And if we leave a message on the machine, does he call back?" The man is shouting.

She puts her hand up to the mask. "But he loves us." she says, quietly. "He says so himself."

"Yes," her husband says, "that's how he signs the thank-you notes: love." Then he looks up at the clock. "I'm not calling."

"But he's expecting to talk to you," the woman says.

Webs flare red in the man's cheeks.

"He'll be home," she says. 'You'll see. He'll answer. It wasn't him down there today." She sets the telephone in front of the man. "He never played with knives. He was such a quiet, deliberate boy. Remember?"

The man's hand sweeps across the table, crashing the phone to the floor.

"It couldn't have been him," the woman whispers, bending to retrieve the telephone and set it in front of the man once more. "He wants you to call," she says and lifts the receiver from the hook. Then in one fluid motion she presses the button that dials her son's number, removes the mask from her face, positions it over her husband's, and places the telephone in his hand.

How the First Family
Spent Mother's Day

In the beginning Cain and Abel saw a balloon in a florist's window that said, "God created mothers because He couldn't be everywhere." Immediately, it started a fight between them.

Cain said," What kind of a God can't be everywhere?"

"You're always so technical," Abel said. "It doesn't mean God is any less wonderful. It means mamma is more."

"Maybe it means the florist wants to sell balloons," Cain retorted, feeling wroth. He hated to be corrected.

And Abel said, "Let's go ask mom why He did it."

And they knocked on their parents' tent.

And Eve was on her couch and said, "Leave me alone. I carded the wool, wove the cloth, ground the maize and made dinner. I don't know where your father is and I'm having a sick headache."

And Abel replied, "But we saw a balloon saying, 'God created mothers because He couldn't be everywhere.' Why did He do that?"

"Men!" Eve sat up and slapped a cold vinegar compress against her forehead. "Always running away from responsibility. Leaving women to take the rap. Nowadays mothers are blamed for everything. Let me tell you, in the old days when He did what He was supposed to do, things were better."

All Cain and Abel had ever heard their parents say about the past was "Life was better in the old country." Instantly they felt guilty, as if they had made this disconsolate woman card the wool, weave the cloth, grind the maize, cook their dinner, and bear them with so much pain.

Your typical dysfunctional family.

Outside Cain felt wroth and punched Abel.

And Able punched him back. Then he said, "Mom has a point. Fifty-two Sabbaths a year we worship the Lord, why don't we use one to do something nice for her for a change?"

"Yeah, we could buy her one of those balloons," said Cain.

"Cheapskate," Abel said. "We'll each get her a present and take her out somewhere swell for dinner."

And Cain and Abel asked Adam to join them and Adam said, "What does your mother do but stay home and have headaches. I, on the other hand, am out in the sun every day. I till the soil, put in the seed, I water, weed and harvest. My back is killing me, but you don't hear me complain."

And Adam entered his tent.

And Eve spoke. "The boys are taking me out for Mother's Day. What are you doing for me?"

"You're not my mother," Adam retorted.

"Yeah?" Eve replied. "If God made me a mother because He can't be everywhere, then God and I are interchangeable. Therefore if God made you, I made you. Therefore I am your mother."

"You're nuts! I was on this earth before God ever thought of you. You were fashioned from my flesh. See?" And Adam pulled up his striped camisole. "If anything, I am your mother."

And Eve's voice grew great. "I will multiply thy pain and thy travail, In pain shalt thou bring forth children," she shouted. "That's what makes you a mother. Pain every month. Travail every year. You were out cold when I got put together. Some mother! You didn't even know what was happening."

And Eve dunked her compress in vinegar again, wrung it out, slapped it against her head, and lay down on her couch.

And Adam paced his fields in the darkness. And he remembered the old country, how glorious his life had been there, wandering from pleasure to pleasure; singing, dancing, eating, swimming, singing, dancing, eating, swimming, And he thought of Eve. How comely she still was when she wore the old, frayed fig leaves in the tent!

And he returned to the tent and he said, "All right, what would you like?"

"Diamonds."

61

And Adam cried out. "Mining hasn't been invented yet."

"Pearls, opera length."

And Adam made a mighty leap and clapped his hand over his wife's mouth. "May the Merciful One above not have heard you," he shouted.

"I'm not going to eat the damn things, just wear them," Eve said. "Go ask a rabbi."

"Rabbis haven't been invented yet either." Adam waxed wroth.

"Oh, for crying out loud," Eve worked up a little wrothness herself. "A mink?"

"That's where Cain gets his acquisitiveness."

And Eve grabbed her compress and turned her face to the wall.

And Adam asked. "How about a nice snakeskin bag? I know where I can get a good buy in snakeskin."

"With matching shoes?" And Eve sat up and her fig leaves crackled.

And Adam saw that it was good.

And he sighed.

And Cain and Abel chose the second Sabbath in May when the Lord usually caused the sun to shine, for their mother's day. And the sun rose and the sun set, and the day arrived. And Abel got a florist to wire him roses and lilies. And Cain had no present in hand. And he led his flock through his orchard, and thought, "Why did I let that goody, goody Abel talk me into this? Everything's so expensive." And here he bent to pick up a Mac that had fallen in his path.

And Cain heard of an eatery where you could get absolutely everything for practically nothing. And it was called *The Garden.* But when he and Abel checked it out, they found a food violation notice in the window, and cherubs with flaming swords patrolling its gates.

And Cain was wroth and kicked Abel.

And Abel kicked him back. But nearby they found an outdoor place on the river Chebar, where the fish was fresh and cheap.

And Cain and Abel arrived at their parents' tent. And Eve opened the tent flap wide. And Abel gave unto her right hand the roses and lilies. And Cain gave unto her left hand the apple.

And Eve was wroth at Cain's gift.

And Cain was wroth that Eve was wroth.

And Cain hit Abel.

And Abel hit Cain.

And Cain hit Abel again.

And they went to the restaurant, and Adam's fish was overdone.

And he said, "I'm not paying a red shekel for it."

So Cain and Abel argued about the bill.

And Cain hit Abel.

And Abel hit Cain.

And it thundered.

And Adam said, "You two stop it!"

But Cain hit Abel..

And Abel hit Cain

And Adam said, "I'm outta here."

And Eve shrieked and stomped off in her snakeskin shoes, "God only knows what's going to become of you two!"

And it thundered again.

Tests

My task is not insurmountable. Just difficult. And one I dislike. I am a tester of men. I record their successes and failures. I spend my waking hours devising questions, interpreting answers, filling tiny spaces with tinier symbols. It is mean work.

I have often thought I could spend my time more enjoyably. Yet I have never tried to change my work. Not that I am without ambition. But always, at the instant I think I can do better, I am assailed by doubts — by the feeling I know no more than my subjects. My subjects are ordinary people, loud, bold, animal-stupid, and so filled with certainty, they frighten me. I am afraid that thinking I am not like them, I am precisely what they are — too dumb to know my own dumbness.

This fear is automatic and controlling like a counter-weight which keeps an object from rising too high. But unlike an object insensately obeying physical laws, I have been altered by it. Old dreams of soaring, of sailing off into unknown lands now rarely rise to consciousness.

Today I am to test my subjects in the arena — all of them at once. This means I will be watched and tested too and makes me more afraid than ever. No one has told me who my judges are or what my test will be. No one has told me what will happen if I fail. I could easily fail. My subjects obey me and answer my questions because they have always obeyed me and answered my questions. They do not know how little I could control them should they rise against me.

I work in a room that is not my own — at a tall, mahogany desk with a pull-down door. When the door is open, the belly of the desk is revealed. It is filled with smooth, deep nooks, too small for my hands.

The rest of the room is furnished with soft, rounded gray chairs and couches. Its tables are silver, its vases pearly and its flowers large, white and perfumed. The room belongs to two women with dark, cap-like hair who dress in black and walk among their furnishings like ravens in a hueless meadow.

64

Whenever I enter that room, it is with satisfaction that I want nothing in it. I keep my books to my chest and my eyes on the floor. This time is no exception. Yet before I reach my desk, I know something is different. From the corner of my eye I see the women smoking cigarettes and pacing. Then I feel another presence. When I follow the women's eyes, I see the man. He is standing apart from them, closer to me. He is tall, solidly built with black hair. I can look at the women or not, as I please, but I turn away from the man.

I try to walk to my desk, but the room air impedes me. It is filled with smoke, perfume, and his breath, which I taste high in my mouth.

I clutch my books tighter. I do not want him. I do not want him to want me. Nothing good can come of wanting.

I have almost reached my desk when he is suddenly behind me. His body presses against mine. His hands cup my breasts. I turn and try to push him away. He holds me tighter. The women's eyes are yellow.

"They will hate me," I say.

"I know," he says.

"I must do my work," I say.

"I know," he says.

"And I'm being tested too."

"Yes," he smiles.

Hotel

She has walked all day.

The hotel shimmers in a hillside garden by the sea. Its low, pink buildings are surrounded by dark green, satin-leafed hedges studded with buttons in color-wheel colors.

They had promised her a room but now there is none. From the pink lobby with its pink reception desk, they send her to the lounge. The lounge is a long narrow room with French windows. No one else is in it. From a south window she can see the surface of the dark and pitted cliffs below. She watches the sea moving in and out between them, lapping at their bases in long tongues with the rhythm of a breathing animal.

When she turns away she is very tired.

By now, the lounge's sconces are ablaze and shadows line its walls. But no one has come in. She longs to lie down. At the far end of the room she sees a pink and green couch. When she reaches it, she finds the green is money. Five and ten dollar bills folded lengthwise and then again in wide Vs, like a barber's open razor.

She doesn't want the money. But the empty silence persists. And soon she is gathering bills and stuffing them into her clothes.

But now she cannot sleep.

There is no one in the lobby — its pink reception desk is bare and the pink cubicles behind it empty — and it reeks of bitter cleanliness. Silently, she creeps down corridors and opens doors. Through narrow cracks she peers into rooms. Here, paisley pillows and yellow lamps exude the sour smells of love.

Outside on the lawn the night is tightly black, the stars large and precise. Nothing twinkles or hides itself from her. For once the constellations are revealed, diagrammatic and discreet.

She lies down on the grass to watch with the others, the people who have rooms. In the dark, the handsomest of them kisses her, but turns away from her tongue.

When she hears a voice, she is too tired to move.

"Well," the clerk says, "you won't be needing a room now."

She doesn't reply.

"It's day," he explains.

She raises her head.

There is no mistaking the tall gray window panes.

The buildings, the hedge and flowers, the cliffs, the sea and sky beyond are flat and colorless.

She nods and starts on her way.

Cold Supper

"Freude!"

As the wooden floor boards of the antiquarian book store reverberated to the last movement of Beethoven's Ninth Symphony, Dr. Ralph Reeseman looking down saw that his shoes and trouser cuffs were spattered with mud. The sight seemed to disturb him. In a moment, however, his attention was distracted. The shop keeper was singing aloud. "Alle menschen werdern Bruder," he crooned along with the radio in a raspy bass voice.

Reeseman glared at him.

"Sorry," the old man said.

The physician didn't answer.

"I can never resist it. Such a wonderful ideas, that Beethoven. Freedom, joy, all men are brothers." The man had an Eastern European accent and rolled his Rs. He was just over five feet tall. A faded, oversize sweater accentuated his slight build and long, narrow head wreathed in straggly gray hair. Reeseman thought the man's accent accounted for his open devotion to oceanic expressions of liberty. He found it naive, but understandable.

Almost at the same moment, however, a disagreeable idea formed in back of his mind. It had to do with singing along with Wagner. But he wasn't in the mood to pursue his thoughts. Instead, he nodded, then looked at his watch.

"You want to use the phone?" the shop keeper spoke again.

"If you don't mind."

"Sure, sure," the old man smiled and Reeseman decided he liked the sound of those Rs.

The phone was at the front of the store. Reaching for it, Ralph Reeseman saw a man floating in the darkness beyond the glass—a tall, getting-heavy, middle aged man, with fashionably cut graying hair, in a custom made suit and shirt. (He had refused initials.)

"Not really all that expensive when you how consider how long they'll last," Anna had said, "and you know how you hate to shop. Besides," smiling, "you look so distinguished." She had exquisite taste in everything. From slip covers to clothes. Everyone told him so.

A sparkling stone in a silk tie, gleaming cuff links, silver eyeglass frames. Against the unfinished shelving and disarray of books suspended with him in the street — a shimmering, incongruous man.

He hadn't spoken to her since the argument last night.

Six around the table at the birthday party Claire Lehmann gave for Hank, and Claire loudly explaining how she had crossed the street when a black man came towards her as she was carrying the cake. "I always do, when I see them. The streets aren't safe," she'd said. "I can't stand it anymore. I'm sure I'll vote reactionary in the next election."

He had been about to respond, when Anna swinging a glass of wine in her right hand after two martinis, her cheeks red and her voice shrill, spoke into the silence. "What this country needs is a good reactionary Democrat. I think my right arm would fall off, if I didn't vote Democratic."

Everyone looked up and laughed. Hank, the loudest. He waited until the laughter subsided, then smiled at Anna and said, "You have the Jewish genetic disease, my dear."

And everyone laughed again.

On their way home Reeseman was silent until Anna spoke, "Why did Hank say that?" she asked. But he didn't answer her question. Instead, he called Hank a cant-filled bastard and Claire a bigot and political imbecile.

"What are you so mad about? What was Hank telling you in the library before dinner?" she asked.

"Nothing," he replied.

"Nothing," she repeated. "Either you don't talk or everything is nothing." And twisting a handkerchief in her lap, she pulled as far away from him as the seat belt permitted.

69

She answered on the first ring. "Where are you?"

"I'll be home in twenty minutes."

He had no intention of telling her he was in a second-hand book shop. She'd ask him to get red bindings to match the drapes.

"Louise said you left the office over an hour ago."

"I can't help what Louise said."

She blurted it all at once."Bobby's been dating a black girl. Claire just called me. She said Hank sees him leaving the hospital with her every day."

She was always like that, he thought, a child who couldn't wait to tell her daddy what had happened at the end of a day. In the early days of their marriage, when she was teaching and came home full of anecdotes, he had found it charming. Now, whether because she had less to say or because he had more on his mind, he found it irritating.

"Is it true?" she asked breathlessly.

"Is what true? That Hank saw him? How should I know?"

"Oh, stop it! You know exactly what I mean. Is that what Hank told you last night?"

"Not now, Anna." He was studying his shoes. "I'm using someone else's phone."

"Ralph!"

"Not now." He hung up.

•

Half an hour later, he was still in the book store. "Hippocrates, Latin and Greek, Giunta, Venice, 1588, with wood cuts," the book dealer said, handing him a thick folio.

Reeseman was not a sentimental man, nor given to worship of any kind. Awe was not in his line. He wouldn't have believed you if you told him he had caught his breath and held it fleetingly before opening the tooled vellum cover of the old volume. Just as he ignored the feeling along his spine and the backs of his arms, as he lifted each creamy leaf between thumb and forefinger, gently, at the top of the page, then slid his hand down the

70

obverse side of the heavy leaf, feeling for the print, almost caressing it, as he placed the leaf carefully against the open cover.

Nor did he realize that he was frowning with the effort of trying to make the rusty residue of his high school Latin unlock the ancient learning.

He would have to restudy Latin he thought turning the pages. There was a pale brown spot an inch in diameter in the center of pages 70 and 71. On 72, 73 and succeeding pages, the spot grew darker, 'til on 78, it was intense enough to look ugly. On 79, it had been removed, a paler disc of ancient paper fitted precisely into the cut and the text matched with precision by an ancient pen to the remaining segments of printed letters. The scribe's once black ink had faded to brick red. For three or four pages the discs got larger and the lettering a bit sloppier as though the penman had grown tired of his painstaking work. Then a new brownish stain seemed to flow upwards from the old one, curving paisley-like towards the spine where it narrowed almost to a point. It too became darker on succeeding pages and ever larger texts were restored more crudely. Reeseman smiled when he saw the last patch, a woodcut, inked in etiolated curlicues by the now totally defeated scribe.

He looked up. The old bookseller nodded. "That's a candle burn." And Reeseman knew he would buy the book. "I could let you have it for a little less."

"Less?" he blurted. Then was blushingly aware that emotion had betrayed him. He would have paid more, the hard-headed doctor, for proof that in his squinting contemplation of Hippocrates' words, he was one with the ghosts of ancient scholars.

•

His right hip ached on every step.

He heard the water running in the bathroom when he got upstairs. Poor Anna, he thought. She was probably expecting him to say it's nothing. Or don't worry, darling, I'll take care of it.

Then she must have heard his footsteps. "It's about time," she called. And in a moment, his sympathy gave way to anger.

"Are you using that oil again? I can smell it out here," he said, emptying his pockets onto the dresser. In the bevelled mirror in its bellied frame, a frightening face. Like the "before" face in the tranquilizer ads. He sometimes wondered how the drug companies got people to look that miserable. Actors with pencilled wrinkles? His were natural. Twin black arcs gouged from nose to chin. Dark nostrils and pursed lips drawn towards each other as if his own saliva tasted poisonous. In a carved gilt frame. The way the Louis must have looked sans powder, heels, hankies and minuets. He didn't fit anywhere today.

"I can't stand the stench in here. I'm going downstairs," he said suddenly.

"Ralph, wait, I'll be right out."

"I'm not leaving home, Anna. For Chrissake, I have to pee."

The book was on the hall table downstairs. He took it into the bathroom and set it on the marble vanity next to the toilet, while he urinated. After flushing the toilet, he put down its lid to sit on it and took the book on his lap. In a moment, his aviator eyeglasses pushed high on his brow, he was holding the book to his face and reading.

Her voice reached him through the door with an edge of hysteria.

"Benny," he had cried from under his bed, searching for the tiny turtle his mother had condescended to let him keep.

"Benny," in a paroxysm of terror for the lost creature, for his about-to-break heart, for the voice he feared high and behind him. "It's your fault. You don't know how to take care of anything."

"Ralph!"

He would hide from his mother in the bathroom, the only room in the apartment with a door that locked. Sometimes he would read in there for an hour before his mother called him. She was a heavy, dark haired women who argued with her neighbors in a high, clear voice. But

72

her voice reached him thin and attenuated through the bathroom door. It had so far to travel. To the river Neva. To Wessex. To Indian Territory.

He never answered. Not until the door knob rattled."What are you doing in there? Answer me when I call you." As if she too feared a voice high and behind her.

After that he would be in her keeping. Not even entrusted to his father. But then, she never entrusted anything to his father. Like a ghost shrouded in a white prayer shawl, his mumbling father had drifted through the small apartment, as if he didn't believe in his own existence.

She was waiting for him in the bedroom, her nails clicking against her mirrored dresser table.

He sat down at the edge of the bed and began unlacing his shoes. The mud startled him again. He slid the shoes quickly under the bed.

She seemed not to have seen them. "Well," she said.

Standing up to step out of his trousers, he thought how vulnerable she looked and felt a flash of pity for her again. She was good. And asked so little of life. Merely for things to match. The impossible.

He dropped the trousers on the white carpet and in his undershirt and shorts, silently stalked to the bathroom.

He didn't see her bend to pick up the trousers and reach for the shoes. But he heard her over the sound of the running water, and of his soapy hands slapping against his cheeks. She was standing in the doorway. "For God's sake, Ralph, is it true?"

He shut the tap slowly and reached for a towel. When he finally looked up at her, his eyes were sunk beneath the ledge of his brow.

"And what if it is?" He said it with his eyes shut.

She caught her breath. "I can't believe it. What are we going to do?"

He glared at her. "Nothing. Leave him alone. He's a grown man. He can do what he pleases."

"You and your leave him alone," she said, then paused. "Maybe it's a mistake. Hank doesn't know Bobby that well."

"It's not a mistake."

"How do you know?"

"Anna, for Chrissake," he shouted, "it's not."

"Don't blow up on me. You're always so damn skeptical. Why can't someone ask you a question?"

"It's not a mistake," he said again.

Her eyes were fixed on his. He turned away. And in an instant, she understood.

"He's a grown man. He can do what he pleases," she sneered. "What did you do, hire someone? No, I know," she went on. "Your shoes and trousers. You did it yourself."

And for a moment, he remembered the mud.

It was dark. He had driven to the furthest corner of the hospital lot — too many people knew his car. He had seen the mud in his headlights as he pulled up and stepped out carefully. In the center of the lot there were tall light poles, strapped together to from a mammoth aluminum trunk that would hide a man. From behind them he would be able to see Bobby's car. He looked around. There was no one in the lot. Walking slowly he reached the lights, then bent casually, pretending to retie a shoe lace. When he looked around, there was still no one in sight. He had some time to wait before the shift was over. Time enough to hear his breathing roar in his ears and to get a violent cramps in his right calf. Time enough to tell himself get the hell out of there.

They were holding hands, his son and the young black woman, when they came towards him, 10 minutes later. Reeseman clamped his lips together and thought of Hank Lehmann's smirk the night before. Then he felt a sudden jolt of pride. His son was young and free. His son had courage.

She was a pretty girl. He watched as Bobby put his hand under her arm, as though to guide her into the front seat of the car. Then she stopped, withdrew her hand and pointed to the door on the driver's side. Bobby left her to

74

open the driver's door, flipped the locks, and she let herself in. Anna always waited to be placed in a car.

Reeseman had no plan. He had somehow thought he would watch for Bobby, then leave. But now, though Bobby put his headlights on, he didn't start the car. Reeseman was trapped. If he moved, Bobby would see him. If he stayed where he was, others might see him. His calf continued to cramp, pulling his heel high. But there was no one in sight. He bit down on his lower lip and decided to wait. His resolve lasted only a minute or two — until he heard laughter, footsteps and voices coming towards him. Then, suddenly, the enormity of his deceit, struck him. The risk or being seen, of having his name called made him almost sick, nauseated. With his head down and twisted away from the lights — it made the pulse that began pounding in his neck, painful — he wound around cars in a broken field run. Not until it was too late and he was already trampling and splashing through the brown muck, at his own car door, did he remember he had intended to be careful. He turned the key, furious at his own stupidity. But driving off, he cursed the hospital for not repaving the spot.

"Big deal liberal. You spied on your son," he heard Anna say.

He sat down on the edge of the bed.

"What are we going to do?" She was still standing.

"Nothing," he said.

"Is she at the hospital? Can you get her transferred?"

"Are you crazy?"

"Then talk to him. Scare him. Tell him we won't let her in the house."

"For God's sake, Anna, listen to yourself. Could you really do a thing like that? And if he says I love her. If you don't let her in I'm not coming in either."

"Oh, Lord," she shut her eyes. "I can't think." But in a moment she recovered. Or the synapses of trivia still functioned. "I should have let Sadie introduce him to that little social worker."

Her response didn't surprise him. His own did. "You're ready to settle for a poor Jewish girl." He was refusing to let her escape. "Why not black? She probably washes and changes her underwear as often as you do."

It angered him. Angered him as it did in the hospital when a derelict, acrid with whiskey and excrement was brought in from the street and the crisp-clothed staff — male, female, black, white, it didn't matter — flaunted their perfumed superiorities. Openly, like coeds used to wear fraternity pins, dangling over their hearts. "You should see what crawled out of the woodwork doc. Yeccch." Not there for the grace of God, not pity, not mercy. None of them looking down to see how far he or she had come. Only up. Up. A moral inflation. Every existence rich with meaning. And life itself, no longer gift enough.

Anna's voice brought him back. "So she washes, why must you be so nasty about it?"

"Because you don't seem to understand that neither one of them is one of your boring slip covers. You can't throw them away or make believe they don't exist."

"It's too bad," she said, clicking her nails again.

He stared at her, not quite believing her last words. Suddenly he was wondering if her nails, like diamonds would cut into glass. Then he felt them, pointed, sharp, digging into his back in the dark and he shuddered.

"Well, find out what's between them," she was saying. "Maybe it's nothing."

His voice ripped from him. "And if he's just fucking her?"

Her eyes widened. "Why are you using such language? What's the matter with you?"

He stood up and began pacing the room. "Nothing's the matter with me. It's you. You want me to say all the nasty, bigoted things you and that Claire bitch can't say out loud."

"Don't call me a bigot."

"Sorry, I forgot your talents. You'd paint the streets white and sweep them every day."

"What's wrong with that?" she shouted. "It's just like you to confuse bigotry with reality. For all you know, that girl's brother could be the one Claire crossed the street to avoid."

"You can be sure, he is."

"And what's that supposed to mean?"

"Forget it." Reeseman cupped his head in his hands. Anna's vehemence had surprised him.

"And let me tell you something else," she went on. "Things like this don't just happen. The Lehmann kids won't date blacks! They had discipline. They went to temple. They went to Sunday school. What did you ever do but talk generalities — be good, be kind, be smart. And you never raised a hand to Bobby. Give him an out, you said. Don't back him against the wall. Let him save face. You do that now and you'll be bouncing your black grandchildren on your knee."

She paused for breath. She was holding herself quite rigidly. When she spoke again her words came slowly. "You wouldn't want him to marry her any more than I would," she said,

He was sitting again, his palms burning against his cheekbones. "No," he whispered.

"Why not?" Anna pressed him. "She washes often enough for you."

"For his sake," he answered quickly. "For their children. For. . ." He couldn't get the words out.

"How noble," she said. "You only think of others."

He felt ashamed. He was thinking of his father again. He, an atheist — when you're dead you're dead. He had never prayed for his father. He could have, but he didn't. And now Bobby didn't even know how. Damn it, he shook his head. But the thoughts persisted.

Ghosts have no right to make demands of future generations, he told himself. I'm not concerned about who Bobby marries, why in hell should I worry about what my dead father would think? And yet.

And yet. Always and yet. Where were these thoughts coming from? Reeseman felt his eyes burning. He had called it integrity not to pretend to a religion in which he

77

did not believe. Still he had considered himself a Jew. Had he been duping himself? Had he been his people's worst enemy? Was there no way to preserve Judaism without religion? Or hypocrisy? Behind Reeseman's burning eyes, Bobby and the black girl were holding hands. And it occurred to him that he may have spent his life doing the most important things wrong.

Anna was right, he thought. It did matter to him. It mattered. And yet, somewhere inside him, there was another voice too. Deep and raspy, it sang, "Freude, Alle menschen werdern Bruder."

He was confused, he told himself. About Bobby. About Anna. Himself. Everything. An iciness shot across his shoulders and his torso twitched. Anna sat down next to him and put her hand on his back. He didn't move. He waited for her to say something. To console him. To open doors. But she was silent.

They sat that way for what seemed a very long time. Until Anna stood up and said, "I'm going down to the kitchen. Supper must be cold. Come on," she took his hand

"You go. I'll be down in a minute," he said.

Without Love

I don't have any trouble believing that Juliet was 14 when she killed herself on finding Romeo dead. Without love, what is there to live for when you are a 14-year-old girl whose parents have used you as an instrument for the resolution of their problems? In my case it wasn't that my folks wanted me to marry anyone as "fair without and fair within" as Paris. If they had, I probably would have said yes just to get away from them. But my parents weren't the Capulets feuding with the Montagues. They were at war with each other. And my mother had her own plan for me.

I can still remember every word my mother spit at me when I got home that Sunday night in September. Until that moment I hadn't known about my parents' war.

My father was a doctor. He practiced on New York's Park Avenue and my mother ran his office. Mother's desk was just inside the front door — a barrier for anyone who might waste father's time and a toll gate for departing patients. The plaque on her desk read, *Ms. Berg*, her maiden name. No one was supposed to know she was the doctor's wife or that I was their daughter. When our housekeeper was ill and I was too young to be home alone, I sat silently in the waiting room. If anyone asked my name, I gave my first name only. If pressed for a last name, mother told me to lie. It didn't happen often, but the terror never left me. I remember thinking my parents would acknowledge everything I could see in that room — the rubber plant, the torch lamp, the black leather couch, the magazines — everything but me.

When I was older, I found it hard to believe that patients couldn't figure out who mother was. Her hair was bleached blonder and curled more crisply than any secretary's. And her speech with its broad *A*s and clicked *T*s, sounded affected — she'd studied diction, had wanted to be an opera singer before she married father. And it embarrassed me to hear her talk to patients about money — the way the cashiers at the school cafeteria talked to kids — no smiles or pleasantries, because it might interfere with her calculations.

Father was cool and elegant. I don't remember his ever raising his voice to anyone. He wore heavy silk ties that caught the skin of my fingertips, especially in winter. The inside of his hands felt smooth arid warm whenever he examined me.

I had spent Sunday at my best friend's — Rita Rubin. I had expected to sleep over and go to school with Rita the next morning, when mother phoned. Rita and I went to the High School of Music and Art, Rita for art, me for music. I played the piano and the flute. Though Rita and I knew each other since I cut off half of one of her pigtails in elementary school, our parents disliked each other. My mother thought Rita's parents' with their foreign accents and relative poverty, were uncouth. Mother believed in upgrading one's self. She had invited Maddy Van Doren to visit me a few times. Maddy had perfect manners and lived on Fifth Avenue. But we had nothing to say to one another. Maddy didn't need me. Rita did. I bought us hamburgers and pizzas, tickets to shows. The first time I returned from an overnight stay at the Rubins, my mother acted as if she had to purge me of a disease. "Don't slouch and don't speak with food in your mouth," she said at the dinner table even though I wasn't doing either of those things. Everything I did that mother didn't like, she blamed on "them." When I blew a bubble that left me draped in pink goo from nose to chin, she pushed me in front of father and said, "Look at that! You've got to forbid her to go over there." But father didn't do it. He gave me one of his pats on the head and said, "Ginny will be all right. Rita and Leonard will be too." Then he walked out of the room.

Leonard was Rita's older brother, a pre-med student in college. My father had got to know him from the times he came to bring Rita or pick her up at our house. There was nothing attractive about Leonard. He was a tall, wore glasses and seemed always to have food in his hand. He ignored me and ostensibly I ignored him. Yet, for a few months when I was 13, I talked more and laughed louder when Leonard was around. There was even a week or two, I managed to bump into him in the Rubins' narrow hallways. It wasn't a deliberate decision on my part. It was as though his presence increased the sense of my own potential — as though if I could get him to notice me, it would mean something good about myself. When he went on eating and walking past me, I hated him.

At our house Leonard would wait around only long enough to find out if father was home. Father would talk to him. Father called him too leftist, but said he was bright and would make a good doctor. He always said it with a little smile and I remember how angry it made me feel. The evening I saw Leonard leaving our house with books clutched so tightly to his side that he looked like an amoeba eating lunch, I refused to kiss father good night.

And there wasn't anything loveable about Rita's parents. In my presence Mr. Rubin complained about rich doctors who drove around in Cadillacs, though my father owned a Ford, and Mrs. Rubin told me that peroxide and permanents "kill the hair."

"I want you home tonight, Virginia," was all mother said on the phone. I didn't get past, "but you said. . ." when I heard the receiver slam. Questioning my mother was a violation of God's sixth commandment.

On the subway, while my reflection came and went in the darkened window next to me, I tried to figure out why my mother wanted me home, so suddenly. The only thing that occurred to me was that she was dying. For 10 minutes, no other hypothesis entered my mind and I was terrified. Partly, I think, because it was a possibility that gave me pleasure. By the time the train got to 125th Street, about half way home, I had decided my uncle Arnold must have died. Uncle Arnold was a dentist, my mother's sister Elly's husband. He was a short, balding man with a brush mustache, who walked with a limp. My mother said Uncle Arnold was sick with a wasting neurological disorder. My father called him a hypochondriac. But that may have been just to upset my mother. I tended to think mother was right, because since the first time she spent a weekend with Arnold and Elly nearly two years earlier, every time she came back from there, she acted strange and remote. She'd gained a lot of weight in the two years, and occasionally evenings, smelled of whiskey.

The first weekend she was gone — I was only 12 then — my father moved out of the bedroom. We had a large apartment on Riverside Drive and father merely began sleeping in the guest room. "You know, I have to work late at night," he explained, "and your mother is such a light sleeper." Father was sitting in my desk chair, while I stood in front of him. He was holding my hand and looking intently into my face. The situation was so unusual, I didn't know where to look until I noticed the heavy gold chain draped across his vest. At the end of it, I knew, was the gold watch with a peaceful face that I used to pull from its pocket, like a full moon rising from the sea. I remembered how the watch lay heavily in my palm, filling it, when I was very small. "You understand what I've told you, Ginny?" father's voice pleaded.

I knew from the look on his face, that he had been saying something difficult to say; something important he wanted me to agree to. But that's all I knew. I didn't understand why it was important. For a moment I was tempted to say so. But then I thought he would get annoyed with me. My father wasn't very good at explanations and he despised stupid people. Only now do I realize how much easier the reputation made his life. Anyway, I nodded, and father sighed and looked relieved, then rushed from the room.

When the train left the 86th Street station, the one before mine, I caught sight of my face again — my round cheeked, baby face. It had disappeared against the white tiled walls, but there it was rushing through the tunnel with me.

A skinny relief elevator operator was on when I got into my building. He stared openly at my breasts and legs. I tried to imagine what he was thinking. The only thing I came up with was a butcher chart. Loin, tender, breasts, fatty. I wiggled my backside getting out, rump, juicy.

Our apartment door opened onto a foyer with the living room just ahead. The dining room, kitchen and pantry were down the hall to the left. The master bedroom, my room, my father's room and a bathroom were to the right.

"Is that you?" my mother called from the bedroom.

"Yeah," I said.

"Yes."

"Yes."

"Come in here."

"I have to go to the bathroom," I pleaded.

"Don't dawdle. I need to talk to you before your father gets home." She came into the hall holding a glass of whiskey.

I had to pass my father's room. His door, tall and white, was closed now. But I remembered an icy winter evening when I had passed it after midnight. The door was open a crack. Father had a carved pink quartz crystal lamp on his desk with a tent-shaped fluted shade that poured warm and heavy light onto a Kashan carpet and made the room's white walls look rosy. I couldn't see into the room, I could only see the edges of the wall. It glowed as if an unseen flame burned within. Twinned, paining odors expanded by the heat of the room leaked into the hallway; the harsh, fruity smell of brandy; raspy, bitter, cigar smoke. Then I heard the low whirring of male voices — my father's sounding like Polonius to Leonard's Laertes.

I cried when I got back into bed.

In the bathroom, I dried my fingers one at a time, until my mother called again.

She couldn't sit or stand. She walked back and forth while I sat in her chintz wing chair with my eyes shut, trying to imagine I was someplace else. It was the place I visualized when I couldn't sleep at night. A boat in the middle of a dark pond surrounded by silver ripples, rocking to the slow triplets of the *Moonlight Sonata*: *Dádada, dádada, dádada.*

She blew out everything in one breath. Father had another woman. From a high society family. Not Jewish, naturally. One of the Toppings. From Park Avenue. The kind that owned horses, wrapped fox tails around her neck in the fall and never wore white 'til July. And she was a model. "It's been going on for two years." Mother's face was red. "It's time you knew the truth."

I was curled in the chintz chair trying to make myself as small as possible. It wasn't time I knew the truth. I didn't want to know anything. I wanted to be invisible. I wanted her words to fly past me. Instead they were piercing my skin and quivering in it, like darts in a cork board.

Mother set her empty glass on a window sill, and spoke to the lights of New Jersey. "After what I did for him. What I gave up for him."

I suppose I should have been sympathetic, but all I could think of was how stupid could she be? If it had been going on for two years, why wasn't she used to it by now, instead of making a scene? Why didn't she find a man for herself and leave me alone?

But she went on about her sacrifices and humiliation, his treachery and greed. The more she complained, the more angry I became. 'Til finally I told her she was a snob. That she was the one always talking about money. That everyone including father's patients hated her.

That stopped her. She came and stood over me and smiled in a terrible way. "Who do you think put me between his patients and him? That kind, liberal, generous doctor himself. Talk to my secretary. She takes care of these sordid details. He never soils his hands with money, Oh no. Not Harry Loehmann. Not unless he's spending it on himself." Then she exploded. "You're old enough to know that your father is a hypocritical, selfish bastard."

I curled tighter, cringed in the chair, and she went on. "He's moving out. Leaving us. You and me."

"I don't believe you," I murmured.

"He won't listen to reason. He won't listen to me." She'd begun walking back and forth again. Now she touched my arm, and I shuddered.

"Go away."

In a burst of fury, she pulled me from the chair and propelled me down the hall to father's door. Neither of us had ever opened it without knocking first. Now, she turned the knob and flung the door away from her as if it were a dirty thing.

It would have been easier for me had the room been bare. There was father's desk, in the center, its drawers open and empty, its surface reflecting the exposed bulb of an overhead light. The pink rock crystal lamp, wrapped in newspapers, was wedged into a carton on the floor. Its fluted shade was in another carton, next to a stack of books. Two paintings and a tapestry leaned against the uncovered studio couch, and there were three sickly gray rectangles on the wall where they had hung. He was going to take the Kashan rug too. It was rolled against the right-hand wall.

Then I noticed a silver frame face down on the couch.

"Go ahead," mother said.

It was a photo of *her* — his lady friend, small-featured, dark-haired, slender in a sleek evening dress. Her arms were slightly forward, as though beckoning.

I put the photo back, walked to the window and like mother a few moments ago, looked across the river into other people's lights. There was everything in that photo that my mother aspired to. Beauty, status, wealth, warmth. Everything mother valued. Everything she could never be.

But none of that had anything to do with father and me. My mother was a stranger my father had married. He had made a mistake. But I was his daughter. Part of him. He loved me. I turned to mother. "He'll take me with him."

But even as I said it, I knew he wouldn't. I wasn't a boy. I didn't have important thoughts, I didn't talk about politics and science. And I didn't have a low voice, a voice like a bassoon that blended with the hiss of cigar smoke and the swish of brandy in crystal glasses.

"He's having these things moved tomorrow. He'll be back tonight." Mother's voice was cold and controlled now. "I don't care how late he comes back. You will stay up and tell him he cannot leave this house. You're the only one who can do it. You will have to insist."

"No," I protested.

85

"Wait," she said, and I heard her footsteps recede.

When she came back, my mother had a paper in her hand.

"Here," she pulled me around to face her. "I've written it all. Exactly what you have to say. And how you have to say it."

Then I recognized her voice and was afraid. It was the voice she used to father at the office when she knew he was going to resist her. The pushy voice of logic speaking to a fool. And I knew I couldn't win. I was too weak. I felt as I did as a child, alone and unacknowledged in that waiting room. All that was holding me together now, was hate. I hated her, hated them both for deceiving me, for trapping me in their lies. For not loving me.

Suddenly we heard father's key in the door and mother jammed the paper into my hand. On legs like melting candles, I ran past her into my room and slammed the door.

I waited, listening as their voices receded into the kitchen, then I opened the door and tiptoed out of the house. I heard mother calling me as I got into the elevator. On the way down, the elevator man's eyes were all over me, but I didn't care.

At first I stood at the street corner not knowing where to go. But then I ran towards Broadway and down into the subway. I rode around for hours, down to Brooklyn, up to the Bronx, sometimes watching people, sometimes crying a little, always feeling alone, 'til I noticed my company — my own baby face. It looked pale and unhappy. It fled when exposed to light. And I wondered if it would ever grow up. Still, it sustained me as I sped back and forth in the dark beneath New York.

The Man Who Sold His Mother

The first time it occurred to Horace Ross to sell his mother, he was having a beer at Charley's place and the idea didn't take hold. Anyone watching the pieces of Horace's face visible in the mirror behind Charley's bottles, wouldn't have noticed any change. The lips didn't smile, the eyes didn't flutter, the furrows beneath Horace's slack gray hair didn't unfurl. So Charley, wiping glasses didn't offer his usual "Wouldn't give no plug nickel for your thoughts." Not that Horace would have told him what was on his mind. Lots of people came to Charley's to cry. Not Horace. He took his beer without salt.

It came from living with her.

"How old are you sonny?" To the delivery boy. Then: "This is my sonny. Give the nice boy a quarter, Horace. When you grow up, you be good to your ma, just like he is."

He kept his mouth shut. Fifty-one years — speak no pain.

The second time the idea occurred to him, he was at Charley's again. This time the idea turned in his head, this way and that like a street woman showing off her wares. His lips twitched and his eyelids rose like theater curtains. And he liked what he saw. What he saw was himself, Horace Ross trundling his mother in a wheel barrow down a country road.

When his eyelids came down, Charley was smiling at him.

After two beers he usually went home. He was on his fourth when the woman sat down next to him. He didn't look at her. He heard and smelled. The kind of woman mother's eyes would destroy in the street.

He moved away.

In a few minutes she was next to him once more. "Are you going to move over again?" she asked.

"I ain't much of a talker."

"The name's Betty."

"From around here?"

"Just traveling through."

He downed the beer, wiped foam from his face, and ordered another. "Horace," he said. "Horace Ross."

Speaking his name set fear biting in his belly. What if she had relatives in town, and mother found out.

"I know you think I'm a nosy old woman." Mother said every time she telephoned when he was late coming home from work. He'd called her that, at 17, when she'd called all his friends to find out the name of the girl he was dating.

"You got folks in town?" Horace asked.

"Uh-uh." The woman shook her head.

"What about your ma?"

"Got rid of her 10 years ago."

"Smart." Horace reached for his beer. "I'm going to sell mine," he said.

"Ma's ain't fetching much these days. Why don't you just kill her?" the woman smiled.

The glass was half way to Horace's parted lips. But he didn't drink from it. Instead, he flung the foaming liquid into her face and fled into the street.

•

It took a month for Horace to be able to show himself at Charley's. He had never acted so angry in his life and all Charley said when he saw him was, "Done blowing off steam?" Horace spent his first two beers thinking maybe it wasn't such a crime to get mad at someone. Then a shouting incident broke out, graduated to shoves and knuckles and ended with spattered blood. It made Horace's heart beat like a steam engine and blew his conscience upside down again.

"I don't mind guys boiling over once in a while," Charley said, sliding a third beer toward him after the cops cleared the place out, "but you take the lid off some of them and they end up killers."

The new beer brought the laden wheelbarrow back to Horace's eyes. Perfect. It was perfect. "Promise me one thing." How many times had she sworn him to the oath. "No matter what happens, you won't stick me in an old age home."

Well, he wouldn't.

After the fourth beer he knew the road the barrow was on. In Vermont. And the type of shop he would offer her to. Mother, it had become clear to Horace, with her birth certificate pinned to her breast, was collectible Americana.

•

When he got home she was up. The arthritis again. "Where were you?" And wanted a back rub. At first he didn't mind. But while he was uncapping the alcohol, the laughter — her sympathetic laughter — began. "You poor boy, the things you have to do for your old mother, because you're lucky enough to still have her. Well, just another few years." And he knew she was laughing because she would never die and he would never be free. Anger spurted inside him and made his heart beat like a jack hammer and his conscience turn over again.

It was easy to get her to go with him. He'd expected it to be. She was too full of the sense of her maternal powers and of faith in the reciprocity of maternal love to suspect ulterior motives. Besides, she liked car rides.

It took two hours to get to the state line. He picked up a wheel barrow in Bennington, jammed it into the trunk and headed east across the state.

•

No one wanted her.

In south Vermont, they told him try up north. In the north they said the hills. No one in the hills wanted a ma. Not even for free. "You can't get back what they cost to feed and repair. No one in his right mind wants to be saddled with a ma these days," a man with a barnful of carousel horses told him.

Horace was panting. It was hot, the road was dusty, the barrow heavy.

Two weeks had passed since they set out. When she was in the car with him, ma talked a blue streak. But he didn't mind because he knew it wasn't going to last too long. In fact, it made the time pass more quickly. He'd drop a pill into her coffee when he had to use the barrow. Once she woke and found herself in it, and to his surprise, it didn't bother her. In fact she said it was nice he'd gotten it, her walking was so bad. For the first time in her life, she said, Horace was showing real consideration. When she'd smiled at him, Horace noticed that her teeth were small and round, like white corn kernels

"Your best bet," the carousel man said, "is closer into town."

In the towns they laughed. The vogue for ma's was over. "Market's been dead three years," a Manchester dealer told him, smiling down at the barrow, and Horace shuddered. "Unless . . ."

"Unless?"

"Heard a rumor. There's a girl buying ma's. Don't know why."

Doc McGowan in the pharmacy was the one to ask.

"Oh, ma's." McGowan was genial. "Like hula hoops. I got stuck with a barnful of the damn things when the fad passed. Figured out a good way to get rid of them, though. Made a tidy profit too."

Horace was in no mood for talk. Mother and the barrow were in the car parked at the curb.

But McGowan went on. "They're hollow, those hoops. Did you know? Cut them up," he chuckled. "For straws. Charged extra for 'em. Made a big hit at the fountain." He seemed about to expand further but Horace interrupted.

"What about the girl who's collecting ma's."

"Yankee ingenuity," McGowan ignored him. "Use all the parts but the squeal."

"What about the girl?" Horace insisted.

"Ain't no one buying ma's today." McGowan's voice dropped.

"I'm not asking much." Horace banged on the counter. "Maybe 50 dollars."

"Ain't no one buying them," McGowan repeated.

Then a sound in the street. Ma had got out of the car and was coming towards the store.

"I heard there is." Horace reached past the silver siphons and grabbed McGowan by the tie.

"OK, OK," McGowan said, breaking free and rearranging himself. He pulled a piece of paper from a drawer and began writing. "Here. It's a white house. Up at the other end of the county. Her name is Missy."

Horace had the paper in his pocket by the time ma reached his side. She was thirsty. He bought her a sarsaparilla soda into which he dropped one of the pills when no one was looking.

Then to make conversation he asked the pharmacist if there was anything new for ma's arthritis.

"Don't need it, these days," ma said, before McGowan could speak. "You're treating me real good."

Horace wasn't sure what ma meant, but it made him mad. He didn't relax until she fell asleep in the car and began snoring again. Looking at her, he noticed her cheeks had filled out. From all the ice cream he'd been buying her, he thought.

•

The house was set three quarters of a mile in from the road. The girl was on the porch — sweeping it — when he arrived. He parked at the side of the inclined path to the house, and leaving mother and the barrow in the car, walked toward her. She was dressed in white, had long straight black hair and wasn't pretty.

"I had a hard time finding you." Horace wiped his forehead. I hear you buy ma's."

"It depends." She continued sweeping. "Who told you?"

"Doc McGowan."

"What condition is she in?"

"A little dusty. We've been traveling, but she still works."

"Why are you getting rid of her? Money?"

"Gosh, no. She don't want to go to an old folks home. And I don't need her anymore. That's all."

"Any relatives?"

"Uh-uh." He shook his head.

The girl set her broom against the porch rail. "I'll take a look."

91

The house was silent. Sparsely furnished. There seemed to be no one else in it. Following Missy's orders, he got ma into the barrow and wheeled her into a large room with only a long, high table at its center. Then he went out to wait on the porch.

In 10 minutes Missy brought the barrow out.

"A hundred and fifty dollars. Just wheel her down the walk and turn left."

"A hundred and fifty dollars," Horace repeated.

"Not a cent more. Look at it this way," she said. "It's a good deed all around. Your ma doesn't suffer and feel unwanted. You get the money. We get a few spare parts." She set the barrow before him. "They'll pay you down there."

Horace's hands closed around the handles. He looked into the girl's face. She didn't smile. She didn't blink. She just returned his look, then picked up her broom and walked toward the house.

Still Horace stared after her.

"All right," she turned before letting the door shut behind her. "A hundred seventy-five."

It took a long time before Horace could breathe. But when he did, the air passed through his lips so quickly, it sounded like whistle.

Black and White

Waking, the first thing the old man saw was the window with the gate across it, then diamond shaped sections of buildings and gray sky. It would snow. He got out of bed and barefoot, with his head down and his right hand at the waist of his pajama pants, shuffled to the bathroom. At the toilet there was a long silence, then a soft stirring of waters. After that the sweet clear chime of a small clock sounded eight times.

On the bare wooden floor of the hall, the old man felt a stab in the sole of his right foot. He stopped and leaned his left hand against the wall and with his right hand pulled a hairpin from the sole of his foot, while his pajamas hung precariously aslant on his hips. Grabbing them, he muttered something toward the doorway and continued to the foyer. From a cracked marble-top table he lifted a piece of paper, held it close to his eyes, squinted, then shook his head. It was no use. He shuffled back into the bedroom.

It was a small blue room, north-windowed and cold: a night table, two-headboarded bed, a dresser and lamp. And all of it was large, dark, grimy and mismatched, yet graceful. His taste. The floor was covered in linoleum. Blue and white squares. Sarah's taste. "Linoleum, I want. You give it a wash and it's clean."

In the other bed, Sarah Rosenthal stirred and pulled the covers up over her shoulder. He reached for the silver rimmed glasses on the table.

In the foyer again, the old man picked up the paper and walked with it to the telephone. He began to dial then stopped. He went into the bathroom. He rinsed his dentures and put them in his mouth.

"Shaugnessy, it's Rosenthal. Yeah, the second-hand man. Yeah, me again." The teeth clacking in his mouth — "Yeah, the store. Sure, I know what time it is. So *what?* You're up counting your money already. Lissen, I'll give you a hundred a month. What are you laughing at? I know you're asking three-seventy-five. You could ask five hundred too. That don't mean you'll get it. All right, I'll

93

give you one and a quarter. Lissen, I gotta make a living too. Agh, you'll never get it. All you rich bastards are the same. It's empty a year already. What do you mean, leave you alone? You're in business or not? I'm making you an offer."

There was a pause. Then the sound of the phone being put down.

"Sonovabitch." And the shuffling began again. He didn't hear Sarah's moan.

He was in the kitchen, the linoleum colder than the wooden floor against his feet.

She knew what he was doing in there. Squeezing two oranges. Boiling two eggs. Toasting two slices of bread. Percolating coffee, his hands deft, silent. She wished he would make noise.

She waited.

She waited 'til she could bear the silence no more. Then, angry-faced, unkempt, wrapped in once-red chenille, she clomped to the kitchen door.

"You didn't flush the toilet."

"I didn't want to wake you."

"And in the afternoon, you don't want to wake me either?"

"It upsets you so much, flush it yourself."

"You forget. You forget everything. You got two pairs of slippers, Anna gave you, you go barefoot. You got new pajamas, you go like a pig."

He poured the coffee carefully, broke the eggs gently.

"And what Ralph said. Salt, you use. With your heart."

He buttered his toast.

"You forget. You're an old man."

"Someone who is married 50 years can't be young."

"What kind of a crack is that?"

"Arrgh." It was a sound between a sigh and a groan.

"You want a younger woman? An old man without money even a dirty slob wouldn't take in her bed. Who were you calling so early?" She stood against the sink. Tightwrapped. Staring down at him.

"It's your business?"

"The Irishman. You pestered him again."

94

"I'll get it. You'll see. He'll come down. It's empty a year already."

"You'll see. You'll see. The same story. Meanwhile 50 years I don't see nothing. So he comes down from three hundred to two. You can afford it big shot?"

"He'll come down to a hundred in a few months."

"Ha! And that'll help you? You can't move furniture no more. Who's going to help you move the junk from the store you got now? Your daughter with the long nails? Your son-in-law, the doctor?" She sat down at the table.

He didn't answer her.

He moved the dishes from the table. Washed and rinsed them. Then he wiped the crumbs from the table. He did it slowly, methodically, silently, as if he didn't see or hear her.

"So he hung up on you?"

He was wiping the dishes, putting them back into the cabinet.

"All right, so don't talk."

He couldn't talk. His eyes, resting on her were round and unblinking. The eyes of a wordless man.

He walked past her quickly now. To shave. To escape. But water didn't mute her clanking in the kitchen. Steel against iron. Tin against tin.

Sometimes his silence sufficed. But not this time. In a moment, arms akimbo, gray-faced in pink chenille, she was standing in the bathroom doorway. "You were screaming in your sleep last night."

He didn't answer.

"Ever since the Blacks moved in, you scream more. Every night. Maybe you should tell Ralph. Maybe you need pills."

She can't tell if he's heard her. The razor's path is straight, unhurried.

For a store, you're looking. For an apartment, you should look, we could move. In this house. On this floor, they moved in, you don't do nothing."

Still he was silent.

"Anna called yesterday. She wants to know how you are."

"Don't do me any favors. Don't tell me any stories. Anna asked about me," waving the razor.

"Who could talk to you? Right away, you're fighting."

"It's a fact. She comes to see you. What does she need me for?" The blade washed — dried — returned to the razor.

"Wipe the sink."

"Ach."

"On top of everything else, you're crazy too. God knows what you have in your head."

White-fisted, he turned and faced her. "How much do you shlep from her?"

"What business is it of yours?"

"It's my business."

"I don't shlep anything. She gives me."

"How much?"

"You wanna know, ask her yourself."

"Go to hell."

"Go to hell. Sonovabitch. That's all you know how to talk." She turned her back on him.

Let her go. The hell with her and Anna. Do I need them? What for? They have no respect. They don't listen. They do what they want. Did Anna take a job, work when he asked her to, when they needed the money? No. She had to go to college. For what? To get married. They ignored him. And they lied. Yes. Sure. All right. Don't worry, poppa. They lied. His whole life, they lied to him. The hell with them.

He went into the bedroom.

In the kitchen she poured herself a cup of coffee and sat down at the table with it, then got up. Sat down again and got up. Let him be upset. He couldn't hold on to money. She took the coffee into the living room. The house was full of junk. In boxes under the beds. Behind doors. And what he liked. The living room rug. Chinese. A crazy color. Violet. Two years ago he came home with it. Two old Negro men carried it in. "C'mon, have a drink." He'd called them into the kitchen. Big sport. What did they

96

have in the house to drink? Slivovicz. Slivovicz for schwarzes.

"What kind of color is that for a rug?" she'd asked him, right in front of them. "Nothing goes with it."

"It's a beauty," he said.

"And it's faded," she added.

"A beauty," he repeated. "Look in the light, how it shines."

But she told him:"Wall to wall is more practical. And more stylish. And the color shows dirt. And it's too thick for the vacuum."

He sat on the floor and stroked it. "See, this way, it's dull. The other way it shines."

Crazy. If she let him, he'd throw every penny away.

She heard him come out of the bedroom. He was dressed. Even in shoes, he shuffled. Black canvas shoes, he wore, in this weather. "Pick up your feet. Where are you going? Business is so good, you're going to the store already?"

The sweet sounding clock chimed nine.

A small, white plastic radio stood on the carved mahogany buffet in the foyer. He turned the radio on to the news, sat down on a chair next to the radio to listen.

"Where are you going. If I talk to you, you don't answer. Or you put the radio on. That's a life? Tonight, I suppose you'll go next door to the Sterns and complain your wife never helps you in the store."

"Shut up! I have to hear the news."

"You have to hear the news. You have to hear the news. I can tell you the news. It's the same every day. The world is going to hell and me with it. Go out. Come back. Don't go out. Don't come back. Who needs you?"

He sat, his face set, grinding his teeth, silent to the end of the newscast.

Did he hear her?

She watched him stand up, reach slowly to the radio, turn it off. She watched him walk to the hall closet, open the door, take a short, black, leather jacket, put it on — "That Nazi jacket you're wearing again?" — and zip it up.

97

She watched him pull the soft, gray fedora on his head and walk to the apartment door.

Then he turned back and eyes squinting behind the rimless glasses, reached into a drawer in the buffet.

She saw something glint in his hand.

"What's that? What is it?"

Silently, he slid the object into his right hip pocket.

"Answer me, you crazy. What is that? It's not enough you have bad dreams, you have to make them come true?"

He stopped near the door, as if undecided what to do.

"Answer me. Answer me."

"Shut up," he said, and began walking towards her, his breath rasping. She backed away from him, holding the robe tightly against her. Her eyes were fiery when he reached her.

He stood in front of her for a moment, stiff-faced, round-eyed, his jaws working. Then, suddenly, he turned and walked quickly toward the door.

She remembered what the object was. A blackjack. He'd found it in that box in the McGuire's attic. "Hit me, go ahead, hit me!" she screamed at his back.

But he didn't turn around again. He pulled the door closed quietly. She heard him lock each of the apartment's three locks. Then his feet shuffled away.

The narrow staircase from the second floor to the street entry of the building zigzagged with a landing between floors. At the head of the staircase, the old man held onto the banister tightly and began walking down. At each step his body leaned heavily in the direction of the leg onto which he put his weight. After two steps, he suddenly stopped. The front door had opened. Looking down the stairwell, he could see a tall black man entering the building. The man passed the mailboxes with their narrow name slots empty as blind eyes — revealing nothing to the world. The old man heard the sound of keys and metallic scraping, but couldn't see anything. In a moment, the black man began mounting the steps. The old man backed silently up the staircase, put his hand to the blackjack in his back pocket and leaned against the wall, waiting. Then he put his head forward and peered down the steps again.

98

He saw white shoes and pants. "A nurse," Sarah had said, when she first told him about the new tenants. "What kind of living is that for a man? He must steal drugs."

The black man was walking up the steps slowly, as if his legs weighed a great deal. When he got to the landing, he looked up quickly, as if he'd heard something; he grimaced and grabbed the banister. When he saw the old man, his face softened. He let go of the railing and stepped back — pausing as though waiting for the old man to come down. But the old man didn't move. Neither man moved nor spoke.

Finally the old man stepped further back and the black man came up the flight of steps. When the black man got to the top, the old man had coins spread in his left hand and was selecting some which he dropped into the right pocket of his jacket. This activity took all his attention and he didn't look up. A subway token fell. The black man picked it up and handed it to the old man. The old man's eye glasses caught the bare bulb in the hall and flashed like mirrors.

"It's pretty cold out there," the black man said.

"Inside this house is cold too," the old man answered and the black man noticed that his eyebrows had long black and gray hairs in them that stuck out in all directions and that his lips were thin. The old man put his money back into his pocket.

"Well, have a good day," the black man said and walked toward an apartment door in the corner. The door opened before he reached it and the old man looked up quickly and put his hand on the black-jack in his pocket again. He saw a red robe and yellow slippers. A young woman's voice filled the hall. "The hot water pipe's busted the super ain't home. I can't take a bath or wash the dishes or anything . . ." she said in one breath.

There was no answer but the sound of the apartment door closing.

Then the old man began his slow descent.

It was snowing heavily and nearly dark at 4 o'clock when the old man walked the long block from his store towards the swaying red neon sign of Burney's cafeteria.

99

The snow was pooling on the brim of his fedora and running off its edges. His gloveless hands were in the side pockets of his jacket, his arms pressed against his body. Under the length of his right arm, he carried *The New York Times* neatly folded in sixths. His sneakers slid occasionally in the slush. His pace was steady, his head down.

He passed a doorway before he came to the window of the cafeteria. He didn't see the three black men in it and he couldn't see through the window of the cafeteria. It was reddish and opaque, streaming with the trails of what might have been thin-blooded tears. Above him, the neon sign creaked suddenly as a gust caught it. Fingers of red light flashed in the folds of the old man's leather jacket and from the black knob protruding from his back pocket.

The three men following him now — one wearing a skull-tight cap pulled down to the tops of his ears — were barely visible except for glinting red eyes and white teeth.

The old man sucked in his breath when he heard their footsteps and turned. They stopped and stared down at him. And when he turned back to push against the cafeteria door, they moved as if to follow him in. He felt the weight of one of their bodies against him as he pressed against the door. "Sonovabitch," he said. It had been the man with the skull cap. But they didn't follow him into the cafeteria. He felt for the blackjack. It was still there.

The old man had to take off his glasses as soon as he got through the door. He transferred the newspaper to his left armpit, reached for a handkerchief in his right-hand pants pocket and wiped each lens with a slow circular motion. Then he put his glasses back on, unwinding the thin end of the wire temples around each of his ears, and looked around him slowly.

The cafeteria was high-ceilinged, cavernous, its floor paved with small, once-white octagonal tiles. It was filled with acrid smells — wet wool, cigarette smoke and stale food. Shards of crazed mirror clung to high square pillars. Sounds — voices, dishes, music — bounced against each other.

Behind one of the columns at a small table accommodating only opposite chairs, two men were bent over a checkerboard. One had gray hair and wore a frayed camel colored overcoat. The other man wore a navy blue jacket and brown cap. The old man walked towards the table, hesitated a moment, looking down at the board and said, "White checkers, pheh."

"They're ivory. They're all ivory," the man in the blue jacket said irritably.

The old man didn't answer, but walked quickly past the men to sit at a nearby empty table. He set his hat on the adjacent chair, opened out his newspaper — it was already turned to the real estate section — and reached into his pocket for a silver fountain pen. Two small black boys ran past him. One, in dark green snow pants and a red sweater — inside out, so the label hung out at the back — stopped at the checkerboard.

"Go way," the man in the camel coat said. But the child didn't move.

"Where's your mother?" the other man said. "I ain't gonna tell you again"

The child ran off.

The old man took off his glasses, brought the newspaper close to his eyes and squinted at it. Then he set it on the table again and began making notations in it. He was making calculations in the margin when the man in the camel coat walked up to him. "Hello, Rosenthal" he said,"still looking for a store?"

"He beat you?" the old man said without looking up. His thin lips curved a little.

"How's business?" the man asked.

"What do you know about business?" This time Rosenthal looked up. But he was staring pointedly at the frayed button edge of the camel coat.

"I had a store 30 years." The man's voice was shrill. "Yard goods. By 167th Street and the Concourse. Some store."

"So how come you're not in Miami?"

"How do you know I ain't going?"

Rosenthal didn't answer, but looked down and resumed figuring, murmuring to himself.

The man in the camel coat, still standing, bent towards him. "My son is taking me down. In an airplane. He flies his own airplane. Maybe I'll have supper with him tonight," he said loudly, then turned and walked away.

Rosenthal looked up again. "Feldman," he called. And when the man stopped and looked back, Rosenthal tipped his head to the side to indicate that he should return.

"I'm looking for a partner," Rosenthal said, whispering.

Feldman sat down before answering. "What kind of partner?"

Rosenthal moved his chair closer to Feldman's. "Your son could put up ten thousand?"

"Easy."

"I got someone wants to sell a patent. A new way to fix china and metal. Then we'll take a store downtown, sell second hand on the side — that's my business now. We'll clean up."

"How much he wants for the patent?"

"What's your business? I'll pay him. Then we'll take the store."

"I'm putting up the money."

"When I see the money, I'll tell you."

"Yeah, but if he asks you too much. You need for rent. To fix a store. You know how much it costs to open up in New York?"

"I can get a store for two, three hundred a month. I'll cut him down on the patent."

"You can't get a store for two, three hundred downtown today."

"What do you know? You looked lately? I got an Irishman, he'll give me for two-fifty."

"How do you know the patent works — he didn't steal it?" Feldman asked. "You could be fooled. Someone once sold me a machine to cut fabric. He stole it. It ripped the goods. Did I have trouble!"

"Can I help it if you're a shlemiel?" Rosenthal's lips curved again.

102

"Lissen, Rosenthal," Feldman said. But Rosenthal's face was suddenly tight. "Sonovabitch," he blurted. He was facing the door of the cafeteria. Feldman turned in his chair. Three black men, one wearing a knitted skull cap, were walking single file into the cafeteria. None of the men looked around. They walked quickly past the serving area and out of sight. "Sonovabitch," Rosenthal repeated.

When Rosenthal stopped looking after the men and his lips stopped moving, Feldman pulled his chair in towards the table again. "You got a lawyer?" he asked.

"A liar," Rosenthal said.

"Come on," Feldman said.

"They're all crooks. I don't need no advice from lawyers."

"You can't go in business without a lawyer," Feldman said. "You gotta check papers, records, leases. It's a big proposition — 10,000 dollars. I gotta know what I'm doin' before I can talk to my son."

"Go to hell." Rosenthal stood up. He folded the paper under his left arm, put on his hat and walked towards the back of the cafeteria. This time his head was up and he was looking around him. He saw the three men at a table. They were pushing something around on the table. He went into the bathroom. When he came out they were still there. A young woman was sitting with them. She had smooth brown cheeks that puffed out when she exhaled her cigarette smoke. Her hair, in tiny pigtails, was ringed with wooden ornaments that clacked whenever she moved her head. She moved it often. The four were laughing and talking loudly and the woman was sitting sideways on her chair, as though she were watching for someone.

Rosenthal walked back towards the table he had occupied. Feldman was sitting where he had left him. Still in his overcoat, he was bent over a bowl of soup. Next to him, in the seat Rosenthal had left, a large woman with white hair, wearing a bright blue crocheted hat, silver-rimmed eyeglasses and large blue earrings, was pulling photographs out of an envelope, thrusting them between Feldman and the soup each time his hand descended.

"This one's the genius," she was saying. "They had him tested."

Rosenthal hesitated, then walked towards the door of the cafeteria.

"Rosenthal"

It was the man with the brown hat and the navy coat. He was alone with the checkerboard set up before him. "You wanna play?"

"They didn't throw you out yet, Bernstein?" Rosenthal smiled, sitting down opposite the man. He put the newspaper on the floor under his chair, took off his hat and put that on top of the newspaper.

"I come back. I have a cup of coffee. Where am I going to go this time of year, the park?"

The black pieces were in front of Bernstein. He made the first move.

The two men exchanged moves quickly. The little boys were running through the cafeteria again. The boy with the inside-out sweater stopped to stare at the board again.

"Get outta here," Bernstein said. "They're all over the place, the little pests. Ain't there no one taking care of them."

The child stepped back, but still watched them.

Rosenthal moved a piece. "He's only a baby. What's he bothering you?" he asked.

"He makes me nervous," Bernstein answered. "I can't think."

"Without him you can't think either," Rosenthal said, jumping one of Bernstein's pieces. He was smiling so that the shiny square dentures showed. He set the checker on the outside edge of the table. The child came closer and stood by his chair for a while. Then, the small, brown hand suddenly reached out, touched the checker and withdrew.

"Scram," Bernstein leaned forward and slapped at the child's arm. "Get outta here."

"You hit a baby?" Rosenthal said.

The child stood looking from one man to the other with his finger in his mouth. He seemed not to understand anything they were saying.

"Come here, sonny." Rosenthal put his hand out to the child. "You know what that is?" He held up the black checker.

The boy's eyes glistened. With his finger still in his mouth, he shook his head.

"That's a checker. A black checker. See? White and black checkers. You put them in the black boxes and you push them as far as you can," he said.

The child didn't move. His eyes were fixed on the checker in Rosenthal's hand.

"You wanna hold it?" the old man asked.

"What's the matter with you, Rosenthal? Them's valuable checkers. He'll run away with it. I'll never get it back."

"Where's he gonna run?" said Rosenthal. "He's a baby." But he put the checker down on the table again.

This time the child reached for the checker and closed his fist around it.

Bernstein leaped up and grabbed him by the label of his sweater. The board fell to the floor. Checkers clacked against the tiles and rolled away. The child began crying.

And suddenly the woman with the pigtails and the three black men were surrounding the two old men.

"It's ivory. It's mine. It's my checker," Bernstein pleaded.

The checker fell from the boy's hand and Rosenthal moved to pick it up.

"Where ya goin', motherfucker?" The man with the skull cap grabbed Rosenthal's arm and spun him around. His glasses fell off and he stared at the dark face before him, his eyes round, unfocussed. There was something he had to do. What was it? What? The blackjack. He began moving his arm around to his pocket but he was inches away when he saw the fist come swinging toward him.

"Sonovabitch," he tried to say. Then he clutched his chest and fell.

The old man was breathing when the ambulance arrived and the medics gave him oxygen. A policeman was speaking to Bernstein who sat near the door with his trembling arms on the table supporting his head which was trembling too.

"How many should there be? I got 18." The lady in the blue crocheted hat straightened up with difficulty from reaching under a chair where she had picked up a checker.

Bernstein didn't answer her. He pulled a large creased handkerchief from a pocket and mopped his forehead, then blew his nose into it.

The police made no arrests. The three black men were gone. The old man had a bruise on the left side of his forehead but he had fallen so suddenly that no one was sure whether he had been hit or had struck a table when he fell.

The medics bound the old man onto a narrow stretcher and carried him out to the ambulance backed in at the curb. Under the neon sign the white paint of the ambulance was red and the red paint, black. The men slid the stretcher through the rear door, anchored it and the driver went around to the front.

"Wait, wait! He forgot his hat!" The woman in the blue hat came running out of the cafeteria waving the old man's fedora and newspaper.

But the men in the ambulance didn't hear her and drove off. When the ambulance with its siren howling got to the middle of the street, its colors were restored.

He was still unconscious when he came back from X-ray and was wheeled back into the Emergency Room. There were stitches in his head but the doctors thought he might have had a coronary as well. The Coronary Care Unit was full. The Intensive Care Unit was full. They kept the old man in the Emergency Room where he could be watched.

Later, while he was being examined by an intern, he awoke sweating and began screaming and pushing her away. The intern stopped the examination and patted the old man's head and whispered, "It's all right. It's all right. We're taking care of you." She had a soft, soothing voice but the old man seemed not to hear her.

106

"All these old guys are the same," a nurse told the intern. "Talking to them don't do no good." The nurse wasn't looking at the doctor. She was looking at the medical resident coming in the door.

The intern used a stronger voice to the struggling old man. "Come on now, Mr. Rosenthal, you can hear me. I know you can. If you don't quiet down, we're going to have to give you an injection."

The old man yelled words the doctor couldn't understand.

The resident told the intern, "You can't give him anything yet. We don't know for sure what the hell is wrong with him. Let's put him in restraints."

"Waking up here would drive anyone nuts," the intern said, looking around the room.

"He's making all the noise himself," the resident answered. "He's probably a screamer from way back."

"Maybe if he saw a familiar face," the intern said.

"Put him in restraints," the resident told the nurse.

Outside the Emergency Room, the intern called a Dr. Ralph Reeseman, whose name was first on the emergency card in the old man's wallet.

Reeseman's service said he was out of town and would call back. When he did call back, the intern felt relieved. He told her he was upstate. He listened to the intern's description of the patient's condition, asked whether certain tests had been done and suggested others. Then he asked the name of the Chief of Cardiology at the hospital and paused for a moment. When he resumed speaking, he told the intern to call the cardiologist in to take care of the old man.

The intern said, "The CCU and the ICU are full. He's in the ER."

"I guess you can't help it," Reeseman said, "as long as he's being watched."

"He's in restraints," she added.

"Why?" She heard the tension in his voice and was glad. Now she'd find out.

"He wouldn't let us examine him. He was fighting us. Is he always like that?"

107

"You'll drive him out of his mind." Reeseman sounded angry. "Tell someone to get his wife," he said. "No, forget that. Wait a minute." He stopped talking to the intern, though she could hear his voice speaking to someone who was probably standing close to him.

"Look," he said when he resumed, speaking hurriedly. "You've got to undo those restraints. Get him a private room if you can. And get a special for him. If the nursing office gives you any hassle, tell them I'll be responsible" He paused again. "He's my father-in-law," he said. "We'll get down there as soon as we can. The roads are pretty bad up here."

"If he saw a familiar face," the intern said again.

The 50th precinct dispatched an officer to tell Sarah Rosenthal that her husband was in the hospital and that they would take her there if she wished.

It was past the time her husband was usually home and she opened the door immediately to the policeman. His badge read *P. Longworth* in letters too small for Sarah to see.

"What is it? What happened, officer?" she screamed.

The old woman looked small, wrinkled and wild to Longworth, as if she'd attack him if he said the wrong thing.

"Nothing serious. Nothing serious," he said quickly. "Your husband fainted over near the Concourse. He's in the hospital."

"Salt, he had this morning, salt."

The officer didn't say anything.

"It's his own fault. What hospital?"

"North Central Bronx. I can take you there if you want."

"He's dead," she yelled suddenly, running her hands through her hair making it look wild too."You'll take me to the morgue."

The officer took out his notebook and showed her the words,"North Central Bronx."

Sarah untied her apron and yanked her coat off its hanger in the closet. With one arm in the sleeve, she wheeled, "Where's my pocketbook?" she said. "Where did I put my keys?" Longworth stood near the buffet in the foyer while she ran from room to room, buttoning her coat and talking to herself.

Suddenly she was standing in front of him. "How will I get home?" she demanded.

"I don't know, ma'am," Longworth said.

"What am I going for? Will I help him? He'll open his eyes and tell me to go to hell."

"Maybe he can come right home," Longworth said, but his words didn't soothe her. The wildness was still in her eyes.

"So what'll I do, carry him? They won't even tell me the truth," she said as if defying him and sat down with her hands in her lap. "They called my son-in-law?" She jumped up suddenly.

"Who's that?" Longworth asked.

"My son-in-law. Dr. Reeseman."

"I don't know, ma'am."

"Sure, they called him. His name was in the wallet." Sarah took off her coat. "I'm not going. I changed my mind. I'll call my daughter and son-in-law to come and take me. They live in Scarsdale."

"It's snowing pretty hard north of the city, ma'am."

"So he'll see me an hour later. What's the difference?" She paused. "This way is better. They can take me and bring me back."

"Whatever you say. You know best, ma'am," Longworth said, wondering if the old lady would change her mind again.

He heard a clock chime once as he shut the door, then the finality of three deadbeats locking into place.

The private nurse found his patient's room, saw that the old man was asleep and went to the nurses station to read the chart: *301/Rosenthal.* He checked on the patient's medication and copied the cardiologist's telephone number into a pocket notebook and returned to the room. The nurse's name was Larry Fitzgerald. He was black.

The patient's body barely made an impression under the bedclothes. The bare skull, fringed with gray hairs was shiny, almost transparent as Saints' feet rubbed worn by too many hands. His face was gray too — a dark, yellowish gray now crusting with white stubble.

The closed eyelids reminded the nurse of those he had seen on tombs. But these were incongruously sunk beneath a ledge of brows thick with black and white hairs going in all directions. The nurse thought he had seen eyebrows like that recently but he couldn't remember where. The left side of the patient's head was bandaged and the skin around the bandage was swollen and discolored.

The nurse made sure the patient's IV was running in at the proper rate — made sure the oxygen was close by in case he needed it. He took the patient's blood pressure and temperature. When there was no longer anything to do, the nurse drew a curtain partially around the bed and pulled a chair up close to it. He clipped a small lamp he had brought with him onto the window sill and began studying a pharmacology text. He read intently, holding the book close to his face to capture the light of the small bulb. Occasionally he put the book on his lap and, using a marker, drew a transparent band of yellow through a passage.

At 11 p.m., a Dr. Reesemen called. He said he was the patient's son-in-law, and asked if the cardiologist had seen the patient. He also asked for some test results. Then he said he was stuck because of the snow. He'd be in as soon as he could in the morning.

At 1 a.m., Fitzgerald felt restless. He opened the Venetian blinds and looked out the window. It was snowing heavily and silently. Four inches of snow leaned against the window. The panes were icy. At his back the nurse felt the warmth of the room and heard air scraping rhythmically from the old man's throat. He closed the blinds, sat down and began reading again.

At 2 a.m., he heard moaning from behind the curtain. He put his book down and listened. The old man was calling someone. Saying mamma or something like that. Maybe it was his wife's name, the nurse thought. He pulled the curtain aside. "What's the matter, Mr.

Rosenthal?" he asked. His voice was soft and thick. The small bulb in back of him silhouetted his head, as he leaned his dark face towards the pale one on the pillow.

Suddenly the old man's eyes opened and filled with horror. "Get outta here! Get outta here!" he cried.

` But the nurse couldn't hear him. He moved his head closer to the old man's.

"Goway, goway, you sonovabitch," the old man screamed.

Still the nurse moved closer.

He saw his patient trembling. Saw his face twitching and his lips moving. He saw his eyes wide and staring and his forehead beaded with sweat.

"What's the matter?" he asked again, moving slowly, gently to lift the old man's head in his hands and wipe his brow. But it didn't soothe him. The old man continued to tremble.

Then it seemed to the nurse that his patient took a long, deep breath, as if he were about to leap at something and his frail body became rigid and tense.

"I'll kill you. I'll kill you," the old man lunged and screamed as Fitzgerald caught him.

Fitzgerald heard only a gurgle – smelled the patient's sour breath — then felt the patient's body become limp in his hands.

"Mr. Rosenthal, Mr. Rosenthal," he called.

There was no answer.

Gently, Larry Fitzgerald lowered the white head onto the pillow and closed Mr. Rosenthal's eyes.

How to Lay a Flagstone Terrace

I couldn't sleep last night, which is unusual for me, especially in the country, where when Arnold doesn't have work to do, we drink a lot of wine and go to bed early. At first I thought it was because we'd just opened the house and it was our first weekend of the spring. Later I realized it was because I'd visited Lily Haberman that afternoon.

Arnold kept coming out of the bedroom asking, "Aren't you coming to bed?" Once he wagged his finger at me and said, "Girls that wanna become mammas have to spend some time in bed." I didn't think it was funny, which tells you about the lousy mood I was in. I even poured myself some scotch. The last time he came out it was 2:30 a.m. He saw the scotch and said, "Well!"

I don't usually drink alone. "I'm not sleepy," I said. "I want to read." So he came over, kissed me on the cheek and went back to bed. Paccy, our Llasa Apso, went with him.

It's strange how certain moments of your life return, always with the same longings, and how even the most bitter taste, tempered by longing, can seem sweet. The acrid smells of this country room — which I disliked: cold ashes, wet wood, mice, mold, were mixed with longing when I was away from them. Winter nights in the city I would suddenly feel them burning high in my nose and wish I were here. I read a newspaper, looked through some old magazines then picked up *How to Do It in the Country*, the book I'd chosen from all those Lily Haberman had offered me that afternoon, because it had a chapter called, *How to Lay a Flagstone Terrace*. Lily was the depressing widow of Bernard Haberman, the United States Appeals Court Judge who had recently died. Lily had been depressing before her husband died. It was thinking about her as much as reading that chapter, that got me out of the house this morning.

I became restless last night though, wishing I could go out right then. I even opened the front door, but came right back in. The door has a small square window at eye level. Through it, you can see the center of the porch and beyond that, where our new outdoor lights reach, the stream and waterfall.

The stream is full now — opaque with soil and foam and its roar is deafening. Even when the stream is low in August, and the water moves in a thin, clear ribbon over the dark spillway, its clatter obliterates all other sound.

I learned about immortality from the stream. But that took time. When we bought the house — it's really an uninsulated added-on-to-cabin in six acres of woods — the water merely charmed us. A brook and a waterfall! Who owned a waterfall? Waterfalls were for smiling smokers in cigarette ads.

I had never been naked out of doors before. I remember I was standing with my arms out and my legs slightly apart to feel the warm air on the inner surfaces of skin that are used to being swaddled or sweaty, when I saw Arnold looking at me.

"It feels sinful," I said and felt embarrassed.

"Come here," he pulled me close to him and down onto the blanket he had spread on the grass.

All our words after that were drowned in the torrent of sound.

Later that night, in bed, I woke suddenly into a terrifying, unrelieved blackness — a blackness I'd never known before. The bed clothing — the ceiling, wooden walls, window glass, the trees, the sky beyond were indistinguishable. I felt Arnold sitting upright next to me. "There's something wrong with the toilet," he said. "It's flushing." He got out of bed and began laughing as soon as he stood up. It was the waterfall.

The stream flowed in darkness and the water fell all that night. It fell all the seconds, minutes and hours of the next day and night, and on through the weekend. The stream was flowing and the water falling when we came back the following weekend and every weekend of the summer. You didn't have to turn it on when you arrived, or off when you left. You couldn't disconnect it or pretend it didn't exist or put a pillow over it to silence it. It was drawn on old maps. It had been flowing past the site of our house for centuries. All that water, all those drops of water — passing endlessly in one direction. Where did they start? Where did they end? Living along the stream we were on the arc of an invisible circle. Could the same drop of water ever come back? Did it matter if it didn't? The stream went on without it. It was the stream that was important — and the circle that gave it immortality. The thought had terrified me. If I didn't have a child, I would be cast forever from its flow.

We'd had our house for two years when Bernie and Lily bought the old Dodgeson estate at the end of the road. We met them when we arrived at the house one Saturday afternoon and found them peering in our windows. They were unabashed. "The name's Haberman, Bernie Haberman," he said, putting his hand out to Arnold. He was stout, wearing bright, red pants, a plaid shirt with red suspenders and carrying a gnarled walking stick. His hair was dyed. Arnold tried to look casual when he heard the name, but I could feel his insides leap to attention. Bernard G. Haberman had just been appointed to the United States Appeals Court by Jimmy Carter. He was a past president of B'nai Brith, ex-treasurer of the Federation of Jewish Philanthropies and National Chairman of the United Jewish Appeal. Arnold was only "a young leader."

"Lily," she said — thin, dry-eyed, with coarse gray hair cut bluntly above the nape of her neck — in a double-knit pants suit, from which her ankles and wrists protruded.

The first time I went up there alone, Lily took me through the house. It was three o'clock on a Saturday afternoon. We carried scotch from room to room.

In the dining room she wet her finger in her drink and ran it across the shining mahogany table, then held it up for me to see. "Clean," she said in her crackling voice. "Good old Hettie. You got a housekeeper?"

"No," I said.

"You will. Someday your husband will make partner and you won't have to lift a finger, like me. But you don't gotta clean now," she shook her head from side to side. "Take it from Lily. You got company — you give a spritz Lemon Pledge in the air and put out lots of flowers."

"Any children?" she asked when we got back to the living room.

"No," I said.

"Me neither. What the hell, they go to California and marry goyim anyway. You work?"

"I quit about a year ago."

"What'd you do?"

"I was a buyer of lingerie for Saks Fifth Avenue."

"I thought at least a school teacher. Why'd you quit?"

"I had a miscarriage, then a still birth. I'm trying to get pregnant again."

"Why're you trying so hard? Your marriage needs cement?"

I didn't know what to say. Why was she asking these awful questions?

"Have him tested," she said suddenly.

"Arnold?"

"If that's his name." She stumped out a cigarette.

When I got back I told Arnold I'd been weighed, measured and dropped into a small box. He said Bernie was smart, tough and told very dirty jokes.

Lily was almost always indoors when I came to see her. Only once, when Hettie was vacuuming, do I remember finding her outdoors — on the terrace surrounding the pool they'd built. She was alone with a volume of the *Encyclopedia Judaica* on her lap, a jug of ice and a bottle of scotch on the table next to her. Hettie brought me out. Hettie was nearly as old as Lily. She had frizzy red hair and wore a white nylon uniform — the kind dental assistants wear.

"Pregnant?" Lily asked me and Hettie stopped to listen.

I shook my head.

"Go cook something, Hettie," Lily suddenly waved her glass of scotch. "Go bake a pie or something."

"The hell with doctors," she said when Hettie had gone. "Jump in the mikvah and pray," she pointed to the pool. "No," she contradicted herself. "The hell with rabbis too."

The first time I suggested to Arnold that we put in a terrace was two years ago when I was pregnant the second time. I pictured myself in a rocking chair, on clean swept stones, nursing the baby and watching the water flow peacefully past us. But when Arnold said, "What for?" I only told him there was no place to put a carriage or playpen because the outdoor surfaces were either rocky or muddy. He said, "We'll see." Nothing happened.

After the stillbirth, I guess, he thought my wanting it would go away. But it didn't. It got stronger. All last summer I sat on the narrow porch sketching in the pad on my lap, visualizing myself on a terrace with white wrought iron chairs and a glass top table with a striped umbrella. I'd be standing at an easel painting — or sitting on one of the chairs, watching the waterfall, drinking white wine — Soave, I thought — from an icy glass.

When I talked about it to Arnold he'd say, "What do we need a terrace for? God knows we don't entertain here. The whole idea of this place is just for us to get away so I can get some work done."

"But it would be pretty," I said.

"Isn't it pretty enough for you? Besides, it'll be something else to sweep and more furniture to take out and put away every year."

"I don't mind. And I could put an easel on the terrace," I said. "The porch is too narrow and the ground is so uneven now."

"You're just unhappy because of the baby, honey," he'd say and kiss me.

I knew he was right in a way and trying to console me. But whenever he said things like that I'd get angry. He made it sound as if my problems weren't real, just the whims of a moody person he had to put with. I was a little fly pestering him. If he waved his hand long enough I'd go away.

At the end of last September, just before we closed the house, I told him I wanted to discuss the terrace seriously.

He was putting it off without knowing what was involved in making one — how much it would cost — how long it would take. He had part of the house where he could work. I wanted a place where I could paint.

He gave me a funny look and said, "OK, later. I want to get some work done."

It was too dark to sketch outdoors. I tried to read but couldn't concentrate. I took Paccy out for a walk and ended up talking to myself — repeating arguments I would put to Arnold.

When he came out of his little room I said, "Shall we talk about it now? We can sit on the porch."

"No, I'm hungry. Let's eat first," he said.

It was Saturday. We had a steak Arnold cooked outside on the grill. The grill was three-legged and tilted on the uneven ground. "See?" I told him, if we had a terrace, it would be level." He didn't answer.

Arnold wouldn't talk about it at dinner, either. He poured Chianti from the big jug into two water glasses, cut a piece of gristle for Paccy and tossed it to her. "After dinner," he said. "I'll make a fire and we'll talk about it then."

While I cleared the table feeling woozy from the wine, Arnold thumped around the living room. "Come on in," he called after a while.

"I'm not done with the dishes yet," I answered.

I was scouring the grill in the sink when he came up behind me. He put his arms around me from behind, pulled the hair back from my face and with his lips against my ear, whispered, "Don't you want to talk to me?"

He had put the lights out in the living room. The only illumination came from the fireplace in which Arnold had stacked the logs vertically. He'd pulled the couch over to fireplace too. The fire was huge. Watching it after we made love, the rising flames seemed to be flowing away from me forever.

Yesterday I'd found Lily Haberman sunk in the leather couch in her husband's study, the huge blue volume in her lap, a glass of scotch shaking in her right hand, a cigarette, dribbling ash, in her mouth.

I had never been in the room before. It had a high cathedral ceiling and a baronial fire place. The walls were lined with bookcases, some now empty. There were piles of books and cartons of books on most of the flat surfaces in the room. The table in the center of the room — dark and heavy – it could have come from an ancient abbey – was heaped with silver — plaques, trays, vases of all shapes and dimensions. The largest was an urn engraved with the UJA logo, Bernie Haberman's name, and inscribed in Hebrew.

Lily was watching my eyes. "Some high class husband I had. That's only the overflow from city," she said. "I got a maid that just does silver." Her words were slurred.

"I'm sorry if I interrupted you," I said. "I just wanted to offer my condolences."

"I'm considering a meltdown. That way I can bury his honors with him. Have a drink," she said.

I poured myself some scotch. There was no place to sit. I felt my fingers clutching the glass as if it would keep me from falling.

"Books are a problem, though. Can't burn 'em. The rabbis don't like that. Take some. They're not all judge books. Take anything."

"Are you selling the house?" I asked, kneeling to look at the books closest to me.

"Cash," she coughed. "I'm getting lots." She took the cigarette out of her mouth. "That's what I like, cash." She looked textureless as a pressed flower — and as sere — as if the next breeze would blow her away.

"What about yourself? What will you do?" I asked.

She shoved her drink onto the edge of the cluttered table next to her and tried to lift the book in her lap. "Volume Nine. In another eight years, I'll be educated." Her laugh was terrible.

I left the house before Arnold got up this morning. When I got back, it wasn't too hard getting the sacks out of the car and dragging them over to the front door. I was reaching for the key in my purse when I looked up and saw Arnold. He was still in his pajamas, sitting on the porch. Paccy was in his lap. I knocked on the door. He didn't hear me. I rapped on the glass. That made even less sound. I knew the waterfall was noisy. But I thought he might look up and see me. I banged again, harder. He didn't move. Suddenly, I was angry. I began rummaging in my bag for the key. Pencils and crumpled papers fell out. I couldn't find the key. I thought of walking around to the other door, but I didn't do it. I decided it was important for Arnold to open the front door. I wanted him to see me. I wanted him to see the sacks of sand I had moved. I wanted him to say, "Hey, what's all this about?" so I could tell him. The hell with the key. I stood at the front door, rattling it. I hit it with my fist. He walked past the window towards the bedroom, holding the dog under his arm, close to his chest.

I hit the door again and rattled the knob. I called his name. Nothing happened. I couldn't see him anymore. I pounded at the door. "Open up. Open up, dammit," I yelled.

Silence.

I bent down and reached for a rock and clenched my fist around it. Then, there he was, coming from the side of the house. He didn't have the dog anymore and he was barefoot.

"Hey, little girl," he said, smiling, "Where you been?"

I pointed to the sacks at my feet. "I'm making a terrace," I shouted.

"How about that," he said, looking at the sacks, then past me towards the car. "You moved them all yourself?"

"I did," I answered. "And I'm going to dig it myself too. I even bought a level."

"How about that," he said again, coming towards me. "Last night you didn't come to bed — you sat up drinking scotch. This morning you hopped out of bed to buy sacks of sand. Where will this end?"

I stared at him. He was still looking behind me and a smile was beginning in his face again.

119

He put his hands on my shoulders. "Where will this end, sweetie?" He was grinning. "You wanna be a mamma or a roustabout?"

He leaned down to kiss me and I turned away. Over my shoulder I saw what he'd been laughing at. One of the bags had broken as I'd dragged it, leaving a wide trail of sand.

"Come on in the house now. Big Daddy will bring this stuff around for you later."

A breeze had come up. Heavy enough to make the stream leap in glittering facets towards the sun. Heavy enough to blow Lily Haberman away.

"Come on, honey, it's getting cool." Arnold pulled me close to him. "Let's go in

"Leave me alone." I shook free. "I want to stay out here."

"OK," he shrugged and went inside. "I'll get some coffee."

I walked as far as I could along the edge of the stream, then sat down, knees pulled up, on a small patch of grass. I stared into the water, not really seeing it, yet every once in a while squinting when a ripple — blinding as the sun — blazed into my eyes.

I was thinking about everything — Lily, me, Arnold, the stream, immortality. I sat there a long time. I don't exactly know how long. All I know is the whole time, I never let go of the rock.

On its original publication, this story was accompanied with a preface on the early feminist movement.

Piazza's Back in the Lineup

Gottfried Lerner, cross-legged on the divan in his Manhattan apartment was playing the flute when the phone rang. It was his mother.

Gottfried felt that mixture of resignation and distaste that often precedes stepping into a cold shower.

"Am I interrupting anything?"

All Gerda Lerner's phone calls began that way. Gottfried was certain his mother imagined him in bed with a model or two. What else would a 37-year-old, wifeless stockbroker be doing home on a Sunday afternoon in the spring?

"I was just playing the flute."

"You still do that?"

"Jesus, it's not like I'm still wetting the bed."

"You should be outdoors at least. How long will it take you to get to Shea?"

"Cut it out, ma."

"Piazza's back in the lineup," Gerda went on, then paused. "So what's up?" she finally asked.

The question irritated Gottfried even more than his mother's directives. She had been counting the days just as he had. Finally, tomorrow, the meeting with Adelaide and her lawyers.

"You know exactly what's up!"

"Good riddance!"

"Ma!" Gottfried's anger flared again. Yes, Adelaide was crazy, maybe certifiable — she'd once broken his arm with a poker — still his mother's easy animosity irked him. Much as he wanted to be rid of Adelaide by now, he couldn't bear Gerda's contempt.

"Will Harley be there?" Gerda asked.

"I can't imagine why."

"God knows what ideas that woman put in the child's head about you. If she comes, it'll be your turn at bat."

Gottfried was holding the flute again. He had learned that by hunching his left shoulder and cocking his head to the left, he could jam the phone to his left ear, freeing his hands to practice fingering. "I don't want an at bat.

121

Harley's been in boarding school so long, she probably doesn't remember what I look like," he replied. "Besides, I'm tired of fighting losing battles. I go to work. I come home. It's quiet. I'm happy."

"Gottfried," his mother drowned out his last syllables. "I will no longer be muzzled."

Gottfried shut his eyes against the vision of his mother tearing off a catcher's mask and dashing backwards to snag a foul. She unmuzzled herself every week in the self-delusory notion that she spent her other days in silence. "I must speak out. You are not just Gottfried Lerner, future divorcé." Here Gottfried winced perceptibly. "You are a father and yes, a son."

"Ma." He felt he was bleating.

"You're sorry for yourself?" his mother went on in fierce tones. "So fight. It will cure you! To just let Adelaide take Harley would be like forfeiting the World Series. Could the child even cope with such a crazy?"

Ma!" Gottfried protested. But once again he was recalling Adelaide's fury — the last of his lost battles — the incident that had precipitated their final separation three years ago. She'd been in one of her dishes-against-the-wall states. Had refused her medication. Everything he'd said or done to try to calm her had made him her target. He'd wanted to flee, but feared for Harley. Finally, he'd gathered some clothes in a suit case and snatched up the sleeping child. The police stopped the car. Assault, battery, kidnapping. Even now, he could hardly bear to think of what had followed: the child taken from his arms, months of litigation — courts, lawyers, social workers, psychiatrists. It's why he'd been willing to pay for the compromise — boarding school. Now Adelaide was insisting Harley live with her — a condition for finally giving him the divorce.

"You're a good looking boy, Gottfried," his mother's voice broke through. "You have a few dollars. If Harley's there, take her out to lunch. Let her see what a nice home we could make her."

"We? Stay out of this!" Gottfried exploded. "There's no we, and there's no few dollars. She's cleaned me out of a house, savings, insurance, everything I'll make for the rest of my life," he shouted at Gerda. "I'm sick of the whole business. I live in one lousy room. I don't need a 10-year-old girl. I don't need anybody."

"You can both stay with me. I would make that sacrifice." Gerda's voice reached him faintly from the mattress where he had dropped flute and phone in his outburst. "One doesn't abandon one's child at any age, Gottfried. Life is not just running away from problems," he heard her more clearly with the phone in his hand once again. "It's a matter of obligation and relationships."

"And I'm sick of obligations and relationships. I've got enough as it is," Gottfried retorted, but in a moment regretted the words. He had thrown his mother a fat pitch right over the middle of the plate.

"I am 68, son. I won't be around your neck much longer."

"I didn't mean you," Gottfried pleaded. But it was too late.

His mother took a deep breath, and in a voice that conveyed triumph, the cheering of fans, and the thwack of a ball headed over the centerfield wall, said, "You want a daughter that hates you? You will be sorry, son, if you turn your back on your child. I am a mother. I know."

"Cool it, ma! Harley's not going to be there."

"So why are you arguing? Promise me only if."

"OK if," Gottfried sighed. He had retrieved the flute and was separating its parts, shaking and wiping them.

"And you'll bring her here for supper afterwards. She should know her grandma again"

"Stop right there."

"I think I'll make a pot roast."

•

The alarm hadn't gone off. It was too late to have coffee. Gottfried grabbed the clothes he'd worn the night before. He couldn't get a cab. He ran the 15 blocks downtown to the lawyer's office, pausing only to ring them on his cell phone to say he was on his way. When he arrived 15 minutes late, panting, sweating, and with his heart pounding, neither Adelaide nor her lawyer were

123

there. He didn't have enough breath to curse out loud. It took him 10 minutes to get it back, and he was thankful to find a newspaper to hide behind. Adelaide arrived shortly thereafter. For a moment Gottfried hadn't recognized her. Her hair was bleached, frizzled and piled on top of her head. She was wearing jeans rolled up to meet the tops of stilletto-heeled boots. "Hello, sweetie," she said and he noticed that her eyes were different too, unfocused, as shiny and hard as the blue Immies he had as a boy.

The lack of an apology, her disregard for being on time, ignited explosions of remembered angers. Gottfried remained silent behind the newspaper, where despite his efforts to dispel the vision, he found himself remembering the night he had fled with Harley. How could a child cope with those icy blue eyes.

The lawyer never showed up. Two hours later, while Adelaide was leaning over a secretary's desk, Gottfried stormed out of the office. He pushed at everything that looked like a button at the elevator bank. Then just as a car opened to admit him, he felt Adelaide's arm slide under his. "I've got a surprise for you," she said, and Gottfried felt an inexplicable wave of fear.

She pulled him off the elevator into the lobby, then suddenly stopped and smiled. "Harley's here. She wanted to see her daddy, didn't you, dear?" She was speaking to a young girl waiting at the concierge's desk. The girl was in jeans too with heavy, laced hiking boots. Her hair was in a pony tail, and she was wearing tiny sparkling earrings. Her eyes met Gottfried's for a moment, then her face reddened, and she looked away. Gottfried wouldn't have recognized her on the street.

"We thought it would be fun to celebrate our impending freedom with a nice lunch at the Plaza," Adelaide said.

"I'm late for the office," Gottfried replied, then turned to Harley.

Color appeared in her cheeks again

"Oh, come on, Gottsy," Adelaide tweaked his arm. "Harley's has never been to the Plaza. She'd love it, wouldn't you, dear?" Adelaide's crazed eyes froze Gottfried's heart.

Harley nodded.

Adelaide was out to celebrate in style — a couple of glasses of champagne, pâté, caviar — if it was expensive Adelaide had an urge to eat it. The champagne didn't mellow her. It settled in her throat. She belched raspy epithets. Diners turned to stare at her.

Harley didn't speak. She didn't smile. She didn't frown. She didn't look up from her plate. Gottfried's head ached. He shrank into his chair and when he couldn't make himself any smaller, disappeared altogether. He stood up, murmuring, "I've got to make a phone call" to neither and both, and left the table.

"You've got a cell phone. You can do it right here," Adelaide called after him.

He walked on.

His mother answered at the first ring. "Just in case you were serious about tonight, I'm not coming for dinner with or without Harley."

"She's there? Two strikes and you walk away from the plate!"

"Look, ma, if there's anything I don't need now, it's insults."

"I'm not insulting. I'm coaching. Adelaide's there too? Listen to me. Be alone with Harley. Away from that woman she could be a different child."

"I don't want to be alone with her. She's a robot"

"She's only 10. She needs a mother! Look at you! You're nearly 40 and still you need me. You know what you should do with her?"

"Who?"

"Harley, your child. Fill her up with love, with fun. It's a shame you can't make it to the game today. The Plaza!" she sneered. "Who knows what that Adelaide told her. Maybe she's afraid of you. Take her someplace for a little girl. Make nice to her. Buy her something. At any age people like to get presents. I'll see you later. I have to finish cooking and get to the game." She hung up.

The sound jarred Gottfried's head. Hit batter, he thought.

When he returned to the table the check was at his place and Adelaide was gone. "Vomiting in the bathroom," Harley's voice was uninflected.

"How are you?" Gottfried asked his daughter. It was the first time they had been alone in three years.

"I don't know," she said quietly and Gottfried couldn't think of what to say next.

The girl was watching the corridor to the bathroom. Her gray eyes were round and solemn — the kind you see in ads that read, *Save This Child.*

What was his daughter like? What did she think of him? What did she know or remember about his life with Adelaide? How would she cope with her?

"Sometimes she doesn't walk too well after she's thrown up," Harley said quietly. The child hadn't smiled all day.

Then Gottfried thought of his boisterous mother with her hits, runs and fighting to win. Well, that wasn't his style. He didn't need to win anything, he told himself at the same moment that he was taking a deep breath as if for a lengthy flute cadenza. "Hey, Harley," he said, and his own voice floating high over his breath sounded unnatural to him, "How about us going across the street to FAO Schwartz after lunch?"

"Us?" Harley was looking towards the corridor again.

"Just you and me," he leaned toward her, realizing how much he had hoped to see her smile.

It was the moment Adelaide returned to the table. "Where are we going after lunch?"

Neither answered.

"No secrets from mommy, now," Adelaide laughed. "FAO, I heard. What did I tell you about how nice your daddy is?"

A waiter appeared at Gottfried's right, and Gottfried reached absently into his inside jacket pocket. His heart almost sprang into his hand. It was empty.

He rummaged repeatedly in it as if he could will his wallet into being there.

Neither Adelaide nor Harley had grasped his situation. Adelaide was lighting a cigarette and staring down the nasty looks around her. But Harley's gray eyes were now fixed on him as if he were the hero at the end of the movie who had come to rescue her.

"I'll be right back," he said.

He knew he had some bills in a back pants pockets, but he'd be damned if he'd count them out in front of Adelaide. The layering and unlayering of cash brought out the bitch in her. He went directly to the maitre d'. By the time he got back to the table, Adelaide was on her feet. "C'mon," she pulled at Harley, "daddy's taking us shopping."

The two singles he had left were now in his right coat pocket.

In the store Harley pulled away from Adelaide to walk alongside Gottfried. Her head came up to his elbow, and he was suddenly struck by her smallness. He reached for her hand.

"Harley, I have to tell you something," he began.

"Hey, wait for me," Adelaide called from behind them.

They stopped at a gum ball machine. "It's just like the one I sent you for your birthday two years ago," Gottfried observed. "Did you like it? Wow. It's over a hundred bucks now."

"Inflation," Adelaide reached them before Harley could answer. "It was only $75 when you got it."

"So what?" Gottfried turned to her.

"It's like our settlement, darling. Things have gone up since we talked business, if you know what I mean." They were facing each other squarely.

"You can sell the house for twice what I paid for it."

"I don't want to sell it." Adelaide glared at him with those crazy Immy eyes. "Harley and I thought you might want to get us something of a personal inflation hedge before we parted." Adelaide waved her hand vaguely. "Down the street at Tiffany's. You know, where they sell all those nice things for girls."

"Tiffany's?"

"You never caught on quick to anything."

127

He glanced quickly down at Harley. Instantly, she let go of his hand and walked off to watch a toy band blast march music from atop a red, white and blue pedestal.

"Well," Adelaide said

Suddenly Gottfried began to laugh.

"What's so funny?" she asked.

"I can't give you or your daughter anything, not even love, baby. You ate and drank too much. I have no money on me."

"There's always credit cards," Adelaide said, leaning on one hip.

"Not today."

"I don't believe you,"

"Left them home. Two dollars," he said almost pleasantly, showing her the bills, then pulling out the linings of his all his pockets."

"In that case, fuck off! Harley," she called and Gottfried's face suddenly went stiff and he felt his heart pounding at his ribs again.

"We're leaving," Adelaide announced when Harley was beside them. "Apparently our visit here was to be purely an esthetic experience. Your father has only two dollars with him."

Harley looked up at Gottfried. "I love the sound of the flute. Do you still play, daddy?"

It was Gottfried's turn to blush and nod.

"And I don't mind just looking. And after we finish looking, we can walk up to Central Park. That's free."

"I am not walking up to any park. We're leaving. Let's go."

Harley stared at her feet.

Gottfried looked from one to the other, and didn't know what he wanted.

"Come on!" Adelaide seized the child's wrist.

Suddenly Gottfried lunged forward and pulled Harley's hand from Adelaide's.

"Make sure she gets home safe, cheapskate!" Adelaide spit into his face.

There is a time of the year of uneasy equilibrium between foliage and sky. It is a time when the full dome of the winter sky no longer glows beyond bare and black trees, but when horizons have not yet yielded place to exuberant verdure. It is the brief moment when branches are thickened, trees appear leafless, and the still visible sky trembles behind a mist of myriad promises.

Gottfried and Harley walked slowly up Fifth Avenue. They found nothing to talk about. When they passed a man selling helium filled balloons, Harley offered to buy Gottfried one. "They're fun," she told him. "And I'm rich. I have my whole allowance with me."

"No," Gottfried replied after weighing the question for some minutes. "I'll buy a balloon for you. I am your father and you are my child and I have to fill you up with good things. That is a moral law. Your grandmother told me so and she's right. It is possible, however," he smiled, "that I may have to borrow carfare from you."

Harley nodded gravely.

Pink, Gottfried learned, was his daughter's favorite color.

A cell phone rang as the vendor tied the balloon around Harley's wrist. Gottfried reached into his pocket, only to find the call had been for a woman standing behind him, and a wave of disappointment struck him. It wasn't until the vendor handed him his pennies in change, that he realized he'd been hoping it was his mother.

Fingering the phone, he turned to look at Harley, but she was no longer at his side. He pushed his way through the knot of people circling the vendor, and frantically called her name. Then he stood still and turned about. People were passing him in every direction. Which way could she have gone?.

He saw the pink balloon first, then his daughter. She had walked up to the highest landing atop a flight of stone steps, and from there had climbed onto a balustrade that ran along the landing. Her right hand, with the balloon attached was around a lamppost. It looked dangerous to him. But Harley was smiling and waving to him with her left hand. He waved and smiled back. Mounting the steps he reached again for the phone in his pocket but in a moment withdrew his hand and was laughing out loud. Ridiculous!

She was probably behind the plate at Shea telling Mike Piazza how to hit.

ABOUT THE WRITER

Writer, poet and translator with a penchant for portraying misfits, Estelle Gilson, was born and educated in New York City. She played the violin at the High School of Music and Art, the viola at Brooklyn College, where she earned a BS degree. Subsequently, and less musically, she earned an MSSW degree from Columbia University and practiced social work in Miami, Florida, and in New York City.

But literature called and over the years Ms. Gilson's poetry, fiction, and translations have won awards and appeared in many books, publications and periodicals. In 1988, while contributing editor of Columbia University Magazine, she received the Council for the Advancement and Support of Education's citation for the "best article of the year." She studied poetry with the late Colette Inez, received grants from the National Endowment for the Arts, the New York State Council on the Arts, the Littauer Foundation, and the Memorial Foundation for Jewish Culture. Her translation of *The Stories and Recollections of Umberto Saba* received the Renato Poggioli, the Italo Calvino and the PEN translation awards, as well as Modern Language Association's Aldo and Jeanne Scaglione prize (1994) as the best literary translation of the previous two years. Her translation of *Separations: Two Novels of Mothers and Children* was awarded a gold medal for translation.

Ms. Gilson introduced Italian magic realist Massimo Bontempelli and literary critic Giacomo Debenedetti to readers of English and has translated from French as well as from Hebrew. Her *Ms. Juvenal* updates the Roman satirist Juvenal's works.

Married to physician-poet Saul Gilson for 54 years, with whom she had two sons, Ms. Gilson is widowed, and now lives in San Diego. In the joyful sunshine of Southern California, she has devoted her time and talents to assembling the unusual population of misfits you will meet in this book.

Ms. Gilson maintains a website: estellegilson.com

ACKNOWLEDGMENTS

Thanks to various publications, where these works first appeared:

A Year in Ink *(San Diego Writers, Ink: 2017):* Haunted

Columbia Magazine (1991): The Man Who Sold His Mother

Kestrel (2000; issue 12): How to Lay a Flagstone Terrace

Magee Park Poetry Annual *(2015):* Here

Other Voices *(Vol. 5, #15):* Cold Supper

Parody: Height of the Delicious

San Diego Poetry Annual:
 Wet at the Gate *(2012-13)*
 Foundlings *(2013-14)*
 You, Anger *(2013-14)*
 The Doll *(2015-16)*
 Spring *(2019-20)*

Stet:
 The Juggler *(#11)*
 Making My Own Movie *(#13)*

The New Renaissance:
 The Moment *(Vol. 2 #16)*
 Why I Became a Writer So Late in Life *(Vol. 2 #16)*
 The Baby's Room *(Vol. 4, #2)*
 Black and White *(Vol. 6, # 2)*

Wind:
 Without Love *(# 75)*
 Handsome Dog *(#77)*

How the First Family Spent Mothers Day appeared on-line.

CREDITS

Cover and **Frontispiece**: *Foundling*
illustration by RILEY PRATO

Other Misfits (page 47):
painting by OLIVIA KALISH

Author:

Back Cover: photograph by SAUL B. GILSON

Interior (page 131): photograph by MICHAEL K. GILSON

Made in the USA
Coppell, TX
03 July 2020